Whispers in the Willows

L. C. Markland and
Leslie A. Matheny

L. C. Markland

WESTBOW
PRESS®
A DIVISION OF THOMAS NELSON
& ZONDERVAN

Copyright © 2015, 2016 L. C. Markland and Leslie A. Matheny.

All rights reserved. No part of this book may be used or reproduced by any means, graphic, electronic, or mechanical, including photocopying, recording, taping or by any information storage retrieval system without the written permission of the author except in the case of brief quotations embodied in critical articles and reviews.

WestBow Press books may be ordered through booksellers or by contacting:

WestBow Press
A Division of Thomas Nelson & Zondervan
1663 Liberty Drive
Bloomington, IN 47403
www.westbowpress.com
1 (866) 928-1240

Because of the dynamic nature of the Internet, any web addresses or links contained in this book may have changed since publication and may no longer be valid. The views expressed in this work are solely those of the author and do not necessarily reflect the views of the publisher, and the publisher hereby disclaims any responsibility for them.

Any people depicted in stock imagery provided by Thinkstock are models, and such images are being used for illustrative purposes only.
Certain stock imagery © Thinkstock.

ISBN: 978-1-5127-2330-4 (sc)

Library of Congress Control Number: 2015920351

Print information available on the last page.

WestBow Press rev. date: 1/7/2016

Preface

Over the past several months I have been privileged to write three novels with my fellow coauthor and colleague Leslie A. Matheny. When we sat down to discuss what we should work on and write next, I offered two suggestions. The first was based more on my own personal experience. It dealt with a pastor who stepped down from the pulpit subsequent to health issues only to fall from grace. It was not until a young man who the pastor helped some years prior that the pastor rediscovers the impact on the lives of those people he loved and served. In all honestly, I opted not pursue that path because it is too fresh and real for me.

The other topic was to write a book describing how people tend to exaggerate and embellish the truth about another without every truly exploring the truth. Jesus clearly declares to His followers to: *"Judge not, that you be not judged. For with what judgment you judge, you will be judged; and with the measure you use, it will be measured back to you (Matthew 7:1-2; NKJV).*

"Whispers in the Willows" is based on this simple statement. The people of a small Midwest town are so ensnared on spreading rumors about an elderly gentleman who lives at the end of a dead-end street, they never honestly take the time learn the history of this old man.

It is not until a young couple moves into an old farmhouse to this old-timer, Woody, that they begin to unearth the secrets of his past and the pains of that past. In the process, they, as well as the rest of the townspeople, come to appreciate "Woody" for all that he contributed to the community, as well as, coming to comprehend the pain he has kept buried for so long.

In the end, the rumors cease, the townspeople rejoice, and "Woody's" purpose to live is renewed and revived.

Chapter 1
"The Weeping House"

In a small town somewhere in the plains of the Northwest region of the United States stood a long lonely road that led to nowhere. It was a dead end; it's name bore the signature of the Weeping Willows that once adorned the street and the house situated on the street's outer most edge.

It was difficult to see it from a distance, but upon careful observation, a person could make out the house that now stood silent and neglected. The house had surrendered and succumbed to the many years of solitude. It was smothered and swallowed by the bushes that once laced its perimeter.. The white picket fence was so worn and weathered that it wasn't even suitable for kindling.

Beyond the house were a ramshackle shed and a small summer cottage. Both buildings were in various stages of disrepair.

In the driveway, buried beneath the brush, sat an automobile. In its heyday, it was considered a sign of wealth. Now it just sat there reminiscing days of old. Its major element to be found on the periodic table for metals was rust. The yard was overflowing with waves of grass that would blow to and fro during a strong wind. So high were some shafts that a person could literally disappear behind its blades. To add to this home that cried for attention were little crosses that littered the lawn: fifty of them to be exact. No one truly understood the purpose for these simple reminders of a tragic event that happened some two thousand years ago, and unbelievably, no one bothered to ask.

In the backyard of this tattered and torn home was a garden. It was simple but of all things, it was kept up. Every year vegetables were seen sprouting from the soil below. Broccoli, cucumbers, cauliflower, green beans, and corn came up during the summer months along with tomatoes.

The house that years ago stood as a testimony of prosperity and joy was nothing more that a tattered shell of a structure. Parts of its roof gave way and caved in to the elements of nature.

The windows that shielded the inside from driving rain, sleet and snow were shattered. They were boarded up with pieces of wood siding that once served as an exterior blanket. Though they afforded some sense of security and protection, they did very little to adequately seal the interior. The plumbing was just as much as issue as the interior. Over the years, water lines succumbed and snapped to the constant freeze and thaw. The only value that the toilet and tub served was for its cast iron. Outside of that, they did absolutely nothing but remind people of past advancements in septic and sewer.

Whispers in the Willows

A person had to be extremely cautious and careful on entering this house of tears. The hardwood floors were so rotten in some areas, it was a hazard for anyone to exit one room and enter another. Pieces of plaster spewed across the floors as if they were remnants of carpet of long ago. The electrical system was outdated and no longer functioned to its full capacity.

People from this remote area called this residence the "The Weeping House." Throughout the years, urban legends ran rampant as people spread one rumor after another regarding both the residence and the person who resided in such an estate of affairs.

Some people speculated that the old man of this house went ballistic having returned home from the battles he fought during the second World War. Others hypothesized that the crosses that lined his yard represented the many soldiers he killed during his time in Europe. While others believed they came to symbolize the many rodents that took residence in this "Weeping House." He killed such animals to sustain his very survival. "They were his form of nutrition," the townspeople would laugh aloud. But then again, there were those who believed this "old man" was nothing more than folklore.

Along this long stretch of road that was nothing more than a dead-end, lived a man's whose life had ended. Sadly, no one ever took the time to discover the truth: to dig for the truth. Most people where either content on spreading the fuel to the flames pertaining to the urban legends that spread like a forest fire, or never did they bother to get to know this old man. There he lived alone along this long and desolate road that ultimately died. And many people truly wished that fate would fall on him. That is, they prayed his life would end like the road his house sat upon.

Chapter 2
"Weeping Woody"

For decades, Woodrow Elliott, known as "Woody" by his fellow soldiers of past, lived alone on that long road that ultimately died at the end of his property. He was an older man and the only time people ever saw him was when he stepped out to check his mail, or when he was in his garden salvaging whatever vegetables that spouted from the soil, or when he would annually walk out into his yard to plot and plant another cross along with a glass jar.

He was a quiet and shy man who learned to live life based on simplicity and solitude. His stature was average and his frame was slender. He had long gray hair with a beard that was of equal length. His eyes were as blue as the sky on a crystal clear day. Regardless of their brilliance, they were also sullen and sunken. The years of seclusion took their toll on Woodrow. His eyes were laced with sadness and lined with sorrow. Though he was considered to be a living soul by the standards of medicine, his spirit had died many decades ago.

He even became accustomed to some of the rumors that spread through the town. At times, he laughed at what people thought of him and about him. There were, other times, he sat by his lonesome and wept. How he yearned to have a friend or two. But, then again, it is hard to dispel one's own legend: especially when it was firmly rooted on a seed planted deep within the hearts of others and watered over the years.

To add to his eccentric reputation were the reports of children. They added to Woody's claim to fame by stating how they heard the sounds of "weeping" during certain calendar events: Thanksgiving, Christmas, Easter, as well as other dates that did not necessarily coincide with any typical or traditional days. Most notably, the day he walked out to stake his claim to the world by plotting another cross in the ground while burying a glass jar by its side. It was from such days and dates that Woodrow would eventually be dubbed "Weeping Woody."

There was a time though when Woodrow was active in his community. In fact, he was quite affluent. He used to own the property that led to his house at its end. It was lined with Willow trees from its beginning to its end. But difficult times hit home and Woodrow was never able to recover from such disasters.

Over time, most people forgot about the difficulties that washed upon the shores of Woodrow's life. They left him to drown in the sea of his own sorrows. Even Woodrow surrendered to the storms that swept him out to sea. He eventually lost most of the property he once owned. He gave up. He failed to pay taxes upon his land. The county therefore was more than content to take over the land that led down his lane.

Preparations were now in the making of developing the drive into something more suitable for the economy. Designs had been drawn for a new neighborhood to compliment the growing population. What no one ever expected was how such plans would ignite the life of an old man who lived at the end of a dead end waiting for his end, and a little girl who provided the fuel for that fire.

Chapter 3
"Park River, North Dakota"

Walking through the back door of his house, Andrew Orr tossed a rather thick packet of paperwork on the kitchen table where his wife sat drinking coffee. Opening up the folio now lying in front of her, she asked: "Park River, North Dakota? Tell me you are joking!"

"No joke honey." Andrew replied. "This offer is too good to pass up." A look of defeat washed across her face.

Andrew was a civilian employee for the Army Corp of Engineers. He was a suit and tie worker that shuffled paper work across his desk in the Regulatory Office in Billings, MT. His passion however was with the land. He wanted to use his environmental engineering background for the good of the soil; not to merely stamp "approved" on applications that came through his in-box. When the opportunity to go into the field arose, he jumped on it.

"Honey, Park River is small town America. It will be a great place for Charlotte to grow up. This is the perfect time to make a move before she settles into school." Andrew went on to justify his decision to accept this offer.

Thumbing through the brochures and paperwork: "What exactly will you be doing?" Marilyn asked.

Whispers in the Willows

"There is going to be a construction boom in Park River. Developers bought a large parcel of land and the town is going through some development..."

Before Andrew could finish, Marilyn interrupted. "Development? I thought you said it was small town America." Marilyn expressed her apprehension when she continued her thoughts by stating. "Honey, development there is like adding a new gas station to go with the only other one in town."

Tired of big city living, Marilyn and Andrew often talked about moving to the plains. Andrew was just waiting for the perfect opportunity to come along. He was sure this was it.

After the birth of their daughter Charlotte, or Charlie as they often called her, Marilyn left her position on the Billings police force four years ago. She enjoyed the simplicity of home life as well as her role of wife and mother.

"Fine." Marilyn whined. "So what exactly will you be doing?"

"I will be a part of the team that will monitor the acreage around the Homme Dam Recreation Area. With the new construction in the town, we are going to keep an eye on the environmental impact. You know, consider the environmental consequences of all building activities and work with the developers to create mutually supporting economic and environmentally sustainable solutions should there be an issue." He replied. "Trust me, you will love it."

"I didn't like it when we drove through there last summer. Why would I like it now?"

"Look on the bright side honey, you will be a lot closer to your parents. Elbow Lake is only a three and a half hour drive from Park River."

Marilyn liked the thought of being closer to her parents. Charlotte would get to see her grandparents more often than once or twice a year. "How soon do you have to let them know?" She asked.

"I already accepted the offer. We fly in on Saturday to pick out a plot and meet with a builder. You can design the house, honey. Whatever you desire, it's yours."

Marilyn didn't have anything keeping her in Billings. Tired of the congestion associated with big city living, she imagined to someday move to the suburbs; but Park River was the kind of town that conjured images of old western ghost towns. It was a very small town with just a little over fourteen hundred residents.

Chapter 4
"Done Deal"

Mr. Clifford had a car waiting for the Orr family at the Grand Forks International Airport. Mr. Clifford was a wealthy man who owned a large real estate development firm. His firm purchased vast acreage that was in and around the small town of Park River. His firm would survey and subdivide the land, and then his construction crews developed residential neighborhoods.

The development of the Homme Dam Recreation Area just on the outskirts of Park River, caught the eye of outdoorsmen. This development sparked interest in the little town. More and more people were moving into the area. Old buildings were coming down. New buildings were going up. Planned development would add numerous new homes to the area.

Marilyn stared out the window of the limo as they passed farm after farm, and field after field. Land was all that could be seen from the road to the horizon. Charlotte fell asleep during the car ride. Giddy and unable to contain his excitement, Andrew took in the smells of the country air and the beauty of the Northwest Territory.

An hour later, the limo dropped the trio on the road next to an abandoned and overgrown cow pasture. A large four-wheeler came zipping across the field towards them. A tall thin man tan with leathered skin and a cowboy hat extended his hand, "Mark Clifford." He said to them. "Hello Mr. Clifford," Andrew said shaking his hand.

"I'm Andrew Orr. This is my wife Marilyn. And this is Charlotte."

"Hello, hello." He said as he tipped his hat. "And this is for you little lady." Handing Charlotte a Dum Dum.

"Thank you!" Charlotte replied licking her lips.

"I am going to take you on a property tour. I will show you some of the features of the different parcels, and then we will head over to the trailer I have on the other side of this land plot. It's about a mile west of here. You decide what parcel you want and we will look at some home blueprints."

The family climbed on the four-wheeler and they were off. Mr. Clifford zigged and zagged across the land. He pointed out rivers and streams that ran across the various fields. He showed them flat lands, and parcels that had rolling acreage. As far as the eye could see. Green pastures, fields of wheat and soybeans covered the earth. As they continued on the tour, Mr. Clifford pointed toward the town in the background. The closer they came to the town, the more houses they spotted. They passed a little country church and an old cemetery.

"What's the big house off to the left?" Marilyn asked.

Whispers in the Willows

"That's an old dead end road over there. The folks in town refer to it as 'Weeping Willows' because of all the willow trees that line the roadside. Road used to end at the cemetery, but some fellow bought the land beyond and built houses back in there for his family… We're talking a hundred years ago or so."

Mr. Clifford continued. "The town bought up most of the land over yonder and parceled some of it off. Most of it is wooded. Can't build on it because of the zoning and Indian treaty red tape. There's an old hermit that lives at the end of the road. His name is Woodrow Elliot. His family has owned the land for generations. He stopped paying taxes on it and the town took it over. There's a property next to him that is for sale. It has an old farmhouse on it. We can head over that way if you want a look-see."

"Yes! Please let's look at it." Marilyn exclaimed.

"The place has been vacant for about a year. It's not in too bad of shape. Mostly the yard needs some sprucing up. Doc Edwards lived there. But he got himself a wife and moved to Sioux Falls.

Marilyn fell in love with the house the moment the four wheeler rolled into the driveway. "This place is perfect!" The white clapboard house was a two story colonial with a porch that wrapped around the entire house. There was a large chimney in the front of the house, and another large chimney going up the back wall of the house. The yard was overgrown with wild flowers and berry bushes. A rickety white picket fence surrounded the yard.

Marilyn liked the large wrap around porch. It would be a great place to stay cool on a hot summer day or stay dry on a rainy day. A porch swing blew in the breeze.

Behind the house were a large livestock barn and a smaller shed. Beyond the livestock barn was a vast field of overgrown grass." Comes with a tractor and mower." Mr. Clifford said as if he were reading Andy's mind. Charlotte spied a swing set and a sand box in the overgrown brush.

"Mommy," Charlotte said tugging on her mother's arm. "Is that a haunted house?" She asked pointing to the dilapidated house next door.

"That's Woodrow's place." Mr. Clifford interjected. "He's harmless and keeps to himself. Once in awhile some of the youth come out and play pranks on him. He doesn't come out much so I reckon you won't see much of him."

"I think we are going to have to move that porch swing to the other side of the porch. I don't want to have to look at that mess while enjoying my summer evenings." Marilyn firmly stated.

"So would you like to see the inside?" Mr. Clifford asked.

The house was so different from the apartment in Billings. The old farmhouse smelled earthy. The wood floors were age worn, but beautiful. An ornate carved banister lined the staircase. The parlor had windows that went from the floor to the ceiling. There was a large kitchen and a smaller summer kitchen in the back of the house.

"This small room off the parlor would be perfect for an office." Marilyn said thinking about a homework space for Andrew. The formal dining room and keeping room had a large fireplace. The house was full of charm, character, and history. It was a century home but had modern amenities. A full bath was added to the first floor. There were four bedrooms and two more bathrooms upstairs along with a sun porch.

After touring the farmhouse, Andy and Mr. Clifford shook hands. "Sold."

Two weeks later, movers emptied out the Orr's apartment in Billings and were en route to North Dakota.

Chapter 5
"At First Glance"

The moving truck backed in the driveway. The Orr's along with the movers hurried to get the truck emptied. There was much to unload and very little time left in the day.

Andrew and Marilyn instructed Charlotte to play on the swing set in the backyard while the adults started the long arduous process of moving their belongings in what would soon be their new home. Marilyn said she would check on Charlotte every fifteen minutes.

Taking Charlotte by the hand, they walked to the back yard. Examining "Weeping Woody's" dilapidated dump, she shook her head in disbelief. She whispered under her breath: "How can anybody live like that?"

"Live like what, mommy?" Charlotte innocently inquired.

Not knowing she was heard, Marilyn politely responded: "Oh nothing, Charlie. I need for you to stay in the yard. Okay?"

"Okay, mommy." Charlotte said jumping onto a swing. "Give me a push please." Charlotte said. Obliging with an under duck, Charlotte went soaring above the scenery. She believed she could almost touch

Whispers in the Willows

the low-lying clouds as she sailed high about the atmosphere.

Charlotte glanced at Weeping Woody's backyard. She could see over the fence that separated the two properties. It just so happened that she caught a glimpse of the man who occupied this eyesore. He stepped out from his back door to make his evening trip to the garden in his back yard.

Hearing the squeak of the swing set in motion, he looked over into the farmhouse backyard. He caught Charlotte's little frame breaking the skyline over the fence. His eyes struggled to focus on the small frame swinging in rhythm like a pendulum ticks in sync with the second hand of a clock. Eyes that once squinted to see rhythmic ticking of the swing, suddenly opened wide as the object on the other side of the fence became visibly clear.

"Charlene. Is that you?" Woody whispered. He went to take his first step off the porch, as he looked hard right. He missed the portion of the porch that was still safe to support any type of weight. He fell face first on the soften soil. Trying to collect his thoughts and regain his bearings, Woody's mind could not erase what he just saw and whom he believed he'd seen. "Charlene. It can't be or can it?"

Woody's mind returned to a time long ago when he started to look forward only to see a pair of little legs standing in front of him. It was Charlotte. Trying to break the world record for heights sailed on a swing, she saw Woody tumble from his steps. The control tower in her little brain instructed that her flight had to be cancelled. She needed to ground her craft to investigate the wreckage from the crash site next door.

Her mother's instructions flew out the window. She had to investigate. She slipped through the broken and battered fence separating the two yards and snuck up on Woody.

She could hear Woody mumble the name "Charley." Innocence was on her side. She had yet to learn the lessons of preconceived presumptions or prejudices. She could remain silent. She extended her little hand to help Woody from the earth he now lay upon and asked: "How did you know my name?"

Still trying to come to find his longitude and latitude, Woody looked up. What he saw was beyond belief. "Was it the fall?" He thought. "This can't be happening." His thoughts became even more jumbled when he looked in the eyes of Charlotte. "No. I must have bumped my head on my way down." He softly spoke.

"Mister. Are you okay?" Charlotte asked.

Reality started to set to the gravity of this situation. This was not a dream nor was he imagining a little girl

Whispers in the Willows

standing before him. He looked down for a second, shook his head and then looked up again. "Charley?"

"Yes." Charlotte affirmed and then asked. "How did you know my name? That's what my parents call me?"

"Who?" Woody asked somewhat bewildered.

"My mommy and daddy. They call me 'Charlie,' you silly goose."

"Silly goose." Woody laughed. "It's been a long time since I heard that saying." He struggled to firmly plant himself on some solid ground. After a moment or two, he lifted his fragile frame from the ground and took his place on the step he missed. All he could do was stare at Charlotte as if he were seeing the Mona Lisa for the first time. His mind traveled back to a different time and a different place. His thoughts broke every type of sound barrier as it blasted to the years that had flown by.

His blue eyes sank along the floor of what is now known as the state of subconscious and were stirred by the muddy and murky waters of the past. His eyes tried so hard to show some signs of life, but Woody had a difficult time separating the present from the past.

His thoughts were interrupted when Andrew broke through the barriers of the old Continental Divide between the two properties. Everyone next door could hear the commotion. Andrew realizing Charlotte was no longer on the swings surveyed the scene. He could see his little girl extending her little hand to this stranger. Andrew charged like an angry bull toward the two.

Most people would introduce themselves to their new neighbors but not Andrew. He immediately took Charlotte by the arm and started to reprimand first his daughter, and then Woody.

"Charlie!" Andrew blurted. "You know…"

He was interrupted when Woody still trapped between the two realms of reality said: "Charley. Is that you?"

Andrew redirected his words on Woody. Though he could tell that Woody was somewhat caught in a daze, it did not prevent him from barking verbal threats to his newfound neighbor. "Look old man!" He blurted. "We have heard about you. You stay away from my family and me!" His threats fell on deaf ears. Woody's thoughts were trapped.

Charlotte tried to be the peacemaker between her father and the man next door. "But daddy, he fell. He needs our help!" She pleaded. But her pursuit for equality was squashed.

In an attempt to drive his point home, Andrew pointed his finger directly in Woody's face and followed it with a warning. "I know you can hear me old man! You stay on your side of the fence and we will stay on our

Whispers in the Willows

side. Understood?" Believing he had just served justice, he snatched Charlotte from Woody's sight and silently escorted her home.

Poor Woody just sat there in silence. His mind was still fixated somewhere other than the present. He was oblivious to the world around.

Out of curiosity, Andrew went to his fence when the sun was starting to set. He looked over and found Woody still sitting on his step. A gentle breeze blew across the yard. Andrew could see Woody's beard and shaggy gray hair being tossed and turned with each passing gust. Temperatures dropped within moments, yet Woody remained perched on his nest.

"Stupid, old man!" Andrew said to himself. In disgust over the details of the day, he angrily turned his back on Woody and entered the comforts and confines of his own home.

Chapter 6
"Do Not Make a Promise You Cannot Keep"

"Honey, we need to get those fence repairs done right away. I don't want Charlotte over there next door. That guy is creepy and his yard is begging for trouble. I should not have agreed to buy this place. I'm telling you Marilyn, we would have been better off going with a property closer to town."

"Andrew, in time we will get to know the man next door. You heard Mr. Clifford say that he is harmless." Marilyn and Andrew stood on the side porch staring over at property next door. Marilyn marveled at what a grand and glorious home it once had been.

Sliding her arm around her husband, "Maybe once we get our place in order, we can see what we can do for him."

Squaring off to his wife, "No Marilyn. Stay away from that codger. I mean it. Marilyn, look at me. Swear to me you will not get involved with that mess and promise me you won't let Charlotte go over there!"

Andrew had no idea what it was like to be home all day, alone. Part of being home with Charlotte was socializing with other stay-at-home families. Marilyn did not want to make that promise to her husband. She wanted a neighbor. She wanted someone that would come sit on the porch and talk about the weather. She wanted someone that would wave over the fence while she was working in the garden. Marilyn was in a bind.

"Marilyn," Andrew's voice boomed interrupting her thoughts. "Promise me."

"I can't. I won't."

"Mommy, Mommy!" Charlotte squealed as she rounded the corner of the porch running towards her parents. "Can I take this to Mr. Woody? Please!" Charlotte was waving a small tin of band-aids at her mother.

Throwing his hands up in exasperation, Andrew walked off the porch toward the moving truck. "You know how I feel!" He yelled as he walked away.

Marilyn picked Charlotte up and gave her a hug. "Bless your little heart. Not right now sweetie. How about you and I head to town to pick up something for dinner?"

Chapter 7
"A Figure Staring Out the Window"

The drive into town was a nice escape. Marilyn loved the way the weeping willow trees blanketed the roadway. The road was dark, quiet, deserted. It was a nice change from big city living. The town was dark, quiet, and deserted as well. Most establishments closed by 8:00 p.m.

"Well Charlie, looks like it is peanut butter and jelly tonight." Charlotte patted her little belly and licked her lips.

By the time Marilyn and Charlotte returned, the moving truck and the moving party were gone. Andrew sat on the porch step drinking a cold brew. Marilyn couldn't help but notice the sharp contrast between houses.

The farmhouse looked so inviting and charming. The soft light shining through the windows served as a beacon to welcome all who entered. The house next door was as black as night. There were no streetlights on their end of the road. The only illumination was from the moon above. Woody's house sat dark: eerily dark.

"I wonder if he has electricity?" Marilyn queried.

"Who cares? It is not my problem." Andrew replied.

Whispers in the Willows

Marilyn took Charlotte by the hand and headed into the house. "Let's go make daddy a sandwich."

After their skimpy meal, Charlotte played in the bathtub while her mother went about making up Charlotte's bedroom. She wanted to make sure that her first night in her new room would be a comfortable night.

Charlotte looked at the pictures while her mother read to her. With her eyes growing heavy, Charlotte said a quick nighttime prayer asking for God to bless her mommy and daddy and even Mr. Woody. Marilyn kissed her goodnight and went to find Andrew.

"What was wrong with you today?" She snapped. "You have been so excited for this move and the job and today you are a different person."

Getting up from the porch steps and hugging his wife, Andrew apologized for his actions. "I'm sorry that I blew up over the guy next door. I can't put my finger on it. I just get a bad vibe."

"I'm going to go tell Charlie goodnight and then I'll get our bed put together so we can have a decent night's sleep. I love you Marilyn. I don't want us to go to bed angry. I'm sorry."

Marilyn sat on the swing that faced the house next door. She wasn't sure, but she thought she saw a figure in the window staring out at her. "I think I'll do some digging in town tomorrow and find out who you are."

Making sure the house was properly secured, Marilyn turned off the lights and headed upstairs. Andrew was already out. He lay sprawled across the bed fully clothed and sound to sleep. Marilyn removed his shoes off and covered him with a blanket. Too tired to draw a bath, she changed into her pajamas and crawled under the covers. This was not the way she had anticipated breaking in their new house.

Chapter 8
"The Job Offer"

Marilyn had a difficult time sleeping. She, like Charlotte, felt for Woody. That evening she made a vow to do all that she could to make him feel welcomed and for him to welcome them. Regardless of Andrew's demands, Marilyn never could imagine someone living under such deplorable conditions or what would prompt someone to live a life of solitude.

The following morning, Mrs. Orr prepared breakfast for her family. Andrew stuck around the house to help unpack boxes and move furniture. Charlotte was content playing on the porch while her parents worked in the house.

With the heavy work finished, Andrew left the house to check in with his crew at the new ACOE office. Wanting to take advantage of the nice day, Marilyn moved her work efforts outdoors. With assistance from Charlotte, they transformed the weedy front yard into colorful flowerbeds. Charlotte picked berries from the shrubs while her mother clipped back the dead branches.

"Let's break for lunch Charlie." Mrs. Orr said wiping sweat from her forehead. Mother and daughter washed up and sat down to another peanut butter and jelly sandwich and a cold glass of milk. Off in the distance

Marilyn saw two boys pedaling their bikes down the dead end road.

The boys rode up on the lawn and laid their bikes in the grass. "Afternoon Mrs. Orr. I'm Tommy Clifford and this is my friend Gary. Can we help you settle in?"

"Are you the developer's son?" Marilyn asked. "Yes Ma'am. He sent us down here to check on you."

"Why that is very sweet of you boys. We are all good here. But if you are looking to make some money, I do have a job proposal for the both of you."

"Ma'am, we aren't looking to make money, we just wanted to lend a hand if you needed."

"Boys, do you see that mess of a yard over there?" She said motioning towards Woody's place. "I would like to hire you to clear that yard." Gary and Tommy looked at one another and in unison "Weeping Woody's place! You have to be joking!"

"Weeping Woody? Why do you call him Weeping Woody?" She asked.

"Look at that place! It cries for help. After you've been here, you'll hear them. They cry!" Gary shouted.

"Who cries?" she asked.

Whispers in the Willows

"Mrs. Orr, trust me." Tommy said. "Kid's voices cry from that house!"

"Oh nonsense." She said sensing that Charlotte was taking all this in.

"Well, do we have a deal? Will you boys work to clear that lot?" She asked. When the Army Corp of Engineers presented the relocation offer to Andrew, one of the incentives was a large housing benefit. Because Andrew purchased an old farmhouse that sat vacant for a year, he did not spend all of the monies allotted to him for housing. He was permitted to keep the unspent funds for home improvements and updating.

Recalling Andrew's words… "You have a blank check Honey. Use it any way you want to make this your dream house."

"Well, fixing up Woody's yard would certainly make my yard more pleasing to the eye." She reasoned.

"How much you paying?" Gary asked. Tommy jabbed him in the ribs with his elbow. "Sure, we'll take the job. We got to clear it with our folks, but I don't think they would mind."

"Alright, I'll see you boys in the morning. Why don't you come around 9:00 a.m? If you work till noon I can feed you lunch before you go home. Work as many days as it takes to get that yard cleaned up." They agreed on a price and the boys hopped on their bikes and pedaled back down the road towards town.

Charlotte went down for an afternoon nap. Marilyn soaked in the tub. Andrew left a message that he would pick up groceries on his way home from work and would be there shortly.

Chapter 9
"Daddy's Home"

"Daddy, Daddy!" Charlotte squealed with delight as Andrew pulled into the drive.

"Charlie, I hardly recognized the place. I almost drove past it." He teased. "You and your mother did a top notch job on that front yard. You can be my land development assistant." He went on.

Marilyn took the groceries from her husband and placed them on the counter. "How did your first day go?" She asked.

"Now that I'm home with my girls, my day has come to a perfect end." He wrapped his arms around her and gave a hug and kiss. Then he gave her a quick pat on the bottom.

Together they prepared dinner while Charlotte set the table. After their meal the family took a walk through the backfield of their property. Marilyn felt like an early pioneer settling in the West. While she found beauty in the barren land surrounding their little farm, she was pleased to know that in time, there would be other families building homes on the outer limits of town. She would not feel so isolated.

Chapter 10
"Operation Woody"

Tommy and Gary showed up promptly at 9:00 a.m. Along with Marilyn, they worked in the morning sun to clear the brush and overgrowth from Woody's front yard. "What if he catches us?" Gary asked. Gary and Tommy cracked jokes at Woody's expense. They filled Marilyn in with all the town gossip about Woody and his eccentric ways.

"What's with all these glass jars?" Tommy queried. Marilyn was just as perplexed. That morning, the trio hauled brush and debris one wheelbarrow at a time. Weeping Woody's yard was taking shape. Charlotte's job was to keep the thermos bottles full of water. She also picked a flower or two and left them in an arrangement by Woody's front door.

After a few hours had passed, Marilyn fed the boys lunch and bid them farewell until tomorrow.

Charlotte went down for a nap. Marilyn soaked in the deep claw foot tub.

When Andrew came home from work that evening, he noticed that Woody's front yard was looking a little less like a jungle. He furrowed his brow, but he did not say anything.

Whispers in the Willows

After the dinner dishes were dried and put away, Charlotte headed for her swing set, while Marilyn joined Andrew who was lounging in a hammock anchored between two trees in the back yard.

"Thank you for this beautiful life Andrew. I love you."

"I love you too." He countered and drew her closer.

Chapter 11
"Operation Woody – Part 2"

Marilyn greeted Tommy and Gary the next morning. After clipping the last bush and hauling a load of debris, they began to transplant flowers from the Orr's yard to Woody's yard. It was Charlotte's job to water the new transplants.

As the do-gooders toiled away, Marilyn sensed they were being watched. But whenever she glanced toward Woody's house, all she saw were curtains moving to and fro. She couldn't tell if it was the breeze blowing through the busted panes of glass, or if it was Woody peering out at them.

With the front yard finished, they moved on to the side yard. "After we get the yard under control, how do you feel about repairing the fence and giving it a coat of paint?"

"Sure thing Mrs. O." The boys replied.

They finished up the side yard shortly after noon. Marilyn fed the boys lunch and offered them a ride home. "I'm taking Charlotte to the church Vacation Bible School registration this afternoon. I'll be going past your house."

The boys declined the offer. "We like to ride our bikes in the evening Mrs. O. We don't want to be without

Whispers in the Willows

them." Gary and Tommy rode towards home. Marilyn and Charlotte soon followed behind them.

The church was a very small building. There were just a few classrooms in the basement and a tiny social hall. Behind the church were an open pavilion and a baseball diamond. There was a small playground with antiquated monkey bars, a big slide, and swings.

Inside the church, the preacher welcomed Marilyn. He introduced her to a few of the Ladies Guild members that were there for VBS registration. They too welcomed Marilyn and encouraged her to volunteer. "I look forward to helping with Vacation Bible School," she told them.

As Marilyn pulled the car into their driveway, she caught sight of Woodrow retrieving mail from his mailbox at the side of the road. She hurried out of the car trying to catch him. By the time she rounded the house to her front yard, Woodrow had retreated back inside his house.

"I'm tired Mommy." Charlotte said rubbing her eyes.

"Lay down on the sofa Charlie. I'll wake you when daddy gets home." Charlotte laid down for a nap. Marilyn picked up a book and headed for the porch.

Chapter 12
"The Storm, The Stare, and the Saying"

Andrew pulled in around five. He smelled dinner the moment he stepped onto the porch. "What are you reading?" He asked taking a seat next to his wife.

"The Winds of Change. I found it in a box in one of the bedroom closets. It's a pretty good story. I think you would enjoy it." The expression on Andrew's face took a drastic turn as he looked out towards Woody's place.

Like a storm coming out of nowhere, Andrew's demeanor went from being a bright day to one that quickly succumbed to rolling cumulus clouds accompanied by thunder and lightning. Hail started to fill their house as Andrew's temper went from bad to worse. It was a side of him Marilyn never saw before.

"Was I not clear about wanting you to stay away from that house next door?" Andrew was angry. Marilyn, sensing that Charlie may be caught-up by the gust of high-speed winds, instructed Charlie to seek shelter in her bedroom upstairs.

"I didn't say anything yesterday about the front yard. But come on Marilyn, I think you need to mind your own business with the guy next door." Andrew stepped off the porch and positioned himself right on the edge

Whispers in the Willows

of the fence that separated the two properties and stared at Woody's yard.

"Andrew!" Marilyn started, but was quickly interrupted.

"How is it possible that you have cleared all the crap out of that yard?" Fuming, he then added, "And where on earth have you hauled it off to?"

Marilyn tried to throw water on Andrew's fire, but it was too late. There was no time for her to grab onto a hose. The damage from "Storm Andrew" had already knocked down power-lines as well as wreaking havoc between the two houses.

"Andrew." Marilyn said in a calm voice. "You are scaring Charlie. Quite honestly, you are starting to frighten me. And what about Woody? I am sure he can hear everything you are blurting out."

She almost had the tornado handled: that is, until she mentioned Woody's name. That only added fuel to Andrew's fury.

"I don't care about that old man." Andrew shouted at the top of his lungs. "For all I care he can up and die in that dreadful place he calls his home!"

Well, there were some things Andrew had to still learn: especially about living in the plains of the Midwest. It was this simple lesson that most people in the area learned over the years. If there is one tornado that rumbles through, then there is usually a second one to roll right behind.

Andrew's high-pressure system eventually mixed in with Marilyn's low-pressure system. The two intermingled right there alongside the "Great Divide." No body was safe. Marilyn had enough. Whereas some may easily categorize Andrew's wind speeds at an F-4, Marilyn's storm speeds blew and flew off the charts.

"That's enough!" Marilyn lashed out. The decibels from her tone seemed to have broken the sound barrier. So much so, that it caused Charlie to look out her bedroom window to see the cause for all the commotion. Looking out her windowpanes, Charlie saw something she had never seen before: her parents arguing. She held her little palm to the window and cried for her parents to stop screaming at one another.

But she was not the only person caught up in this wind tunnel. Woody also heard the whistle from the winds outside. They practically forced him to leave his place of safety.

The shouting between the storms stopped when Woody appeared on his front steps. He cautiously crept off his porch and approached the two frontal systems as their tails started to dissipate back into the clouds above. He did something the neither one of them expected. He spoke.

Whispers in the Willows

"I'm sorry if I created such a ruckus between you two." He kindly said. "I do appreciate everything you have done for me."

Marilyn smiled and reciprocated his words of kindness with: "You are welcome Woody."

For the first time in such a long time, someone finally showed some respect for this old man. Andrew's temper cooled down but was rapidly rekindled when he caught Woody looking up towards Charlie's window. Andrew turned his head 90 degrees only to see his little girl holding her hand against the window. He could tell she was crying.

"You almost had me old man!" Both Marilyn and Woody could see the blood begin to boil again within Andrew's heart. "You stay away from me and family! You hear me!" With that Andrew stormed into the house.

On his way in, he caught a glimpse of the novel Marilyn started to read. The caption on the cover captured his attention. It read: *"Blessed are the peacemakers."* He snorted at the thought and finished storming through his front door.

Andrew in his anger left Marilyn standing outside with Woody.

"Ma'am!" Woody politely said. "I am not worth fighting over. You go inside and make it right with your husband."

"Woody." Marilyn said apologetically. "It's not your fault. Andrew is one of the most caring men I know." She started to cry as her adrenaline returned to its original equilibrium. "I don't know what has gotten into him as of late."

Woody countered her tears with tears of his. "Ma'am. You never know what tomorrow may hold. But I will say that you don't want this to be the way you should have to remember your husband."

He then extended his hand over the fence. He handed her a jar. "Here is a little something for your troubles," he said. Woody then did an about-face and disappeared into the depths of his dwelling.

Marilyn was not about to argue with Woody. She stood silent for a few moments before returning to her perch. She stayed there hoping Andrew would be more reasonable after his shower. Marilyn looked over Woody's yard rather proudly. She caught Woody glancing out of a window. She gave him a wave. He reciprocated with a salute.

With the glass jar still clinging in her hands, Marilyn opted to open it. She fell out of her chair when she studied its contents. In it was a photograph of decades past. It was a portrait of a young man holding onto a little girl while he had his right arm draped around a woman. There was a striking resemblance between the little girl in the picture and Charlie. They were standing

Whispers in the Willows

in front of a sedan that was considered to be a luxury vehicle for its times.

If that was not enough, Marilyn discovered that the photograph was not the only content of the jar. With the photograph was a wad of money: $5,000.00 to be exact. She sat there in silence. Her intuition told her that there was more to Woody than what most people possibly imagined. Her moment of solitude was shattered as Charlie stepped onto the porch and sat in her mother's lap.

She flung her arms around her mother and comforted her with the words: "Everything will be okay Mommy! I just know it." She happened to look down to see the picture sitting next to her mother. "Look Mommy!" She yelled. "That's me in the picture!"

Dinner was quiet an affair that night. Marilyn felt a little guilty, but she never did make the promise to stay away from Woody's yard. She was more determined that ever to reach out to the "old man" next door. She could only hope that Andrew in time would come around.

Chapter 13
"Sacred Ground"

The early morning sun broke the horizon sparking on a new day. For most townspeople, it was another typical day. Had they known of the storm that brewed down the Willows the night before, they would have more reason to add to the existing rumors running through the streets. Yes, the kettle was being stirred again as Tommy and Gary continued to ride their bikes everyday down that long lane known as the "Weeping Willows."

Andrew came down from the bedroom. He knew he crossed several lines the previous evening. How could he forget? Marilyn made it a point to remind him by camping out on the sofa. On top of her was Charlie. Not to disturb them from their rest, Andrew made every attempt to sneak out of the house.

Quietly, he snuck up on Marilyn to kiss her on the forehead. Bending over, his eyes caught a glimpse of the picture clinging in Charlie's hand. He could not make out all of the details since her little thumb covered a portion of this snapshot in time. But what he did see sent him taking a step or two back.

He, like Marilyn and Charlie, saw an exact replicate of Charlie sitting comfortably and complacently in some stranger's arms. He shook his head and countered it with a double take. Stepping back, he inadvertently

Whispers in the Willows

tripped over the end table resting at the sofa's end. It startled Marilyn. From there it was nothing more than a domino effect.

Andrew tried to catch the lamp as it made its descent to the floor and Marilyn jumped to her feet, all the while, trying to snatch Charlie as she went sailing to the surface below. Before he knew it, his best efforts to leave the house in a state of peace and tranquility proved futile.

Everybody was now awake. Despite how the day started out at the Orr house, it did help melt some of the ice that formed from the hail that fell before the torrential rains and tornado swept through their home some hours prior. They chuckled at their own clumsiness.

After a good laugh, Andrew and Marilyn mended the fence that snapped from one another's wrath. Apologies were said, kisses were shared, and tears were shed. All was right with the world.

Andrew made his way to the car. Backing out of the drive he could not help but take notice of two teens riding their bikes down this dead-end road. He knew what they were coming to do. Though he was not exactly in favor of their deeds, he knew not to do or say anything to thwart their efforts. His attention was more distracted on the picture he saw in Charlie's hand.

Driving down the lane, Andrew noticed how Weeping Willows lined the street. He never quite noticed it before.

He looked in his rearview mirror. Sure he saw the two boys riding their bikes toward his house, but that was not the only thing he saw. "Weeping Woody's" house stood in full view. For some strange reason, Andrew knew that there was a correlation between the picture clutched in Charlie's hand and "the old man" he so utterly despised.

It was then that Andrew decided to visit the local library after work to see what dirt he could dig up on Woody. He smiled at the thought. He defined his mission as an archaeological dig on some "sacred ground." What he was soon to unearth would change his definition of this old man that led a dead end life on a dead end lane. It would also change the direction Andrew would take in redefining this man of urban legend.

But, in the meantime, that was not the only sacred ground to be dug up that day. Both Tom and Gary made their way to Mrs. O's. She gave them explicit instructions to begin working on Woody's back yard and if time permitted to start cleaning up what some believed to be a "pet cemetery."

Tommy and Gary did as Mrs. O had asked. They walked toward Woody's back yard only to discover a garden beyond belief. Every row of every vegetable was carefully plotted in this plot of land. They were in perfect rows. Every plant was evenly spaced between one another and was perfectly divided according to the vegetables planted.

Whispers in the Willows

Gary shook his head in disbelief. "How is it that a person could allow his house to fall to pieces, yet have everything so perfect in his garden?"

"It beats me!" Tommy added. "But Mrs. O. wants us to work on his garden."

"There is nothing to do here." Gary said. "Hey! I have an idea."

"I don't know. Every time you tell me you have an idea, we seem to get into trouble." Tommy added.

"That's not true." Gary argued. "And besides, my idea goes in line with what Mrs. O. has asked us to do."

"Let me guess." Tom said sarcastically. "You want to go over to the 'pet cemetery' I bet."

"How did you know?"

"Because you are too predictable." Tommy said smiling. "I agree with you. Let's see what's underneath those crosses."

"I bet we will find corpses of every kind of animal known to our region." Gary busted out with great enthusiasm.

"Who knows? Maybe we will find human remains. Wouldn't that be so cool?" Tommy added to the possibilities.

"Tommy, why do you have to ruin this?" Gary hesitantly asked. "Human remains? Seriously?"

Encouraging Gary to press forward, Tommy went on to add: "Oh! Quit being such a wimp. Just think of the tales we can tell if we find something! We will be heroes!"

Both boys headed to the yard of crosses. As they proceeded on their adventure, they discussed all the possibilities of what could happen. They could see reporters from across the nation interviewing them as to the uncovered remains from who knows what. They laughed at the thought. To be famous was more than they could ever imagine.

Their dreams for a bigger and brighter day were dashed even before they could begin to disturb the soil from which they were about to dig. As soon as the spade of the shovel touched the soil, old man Woody appeared from nowhere.

Tommy looked at Gary in disbelief. "I told you this was a bad idea. I should have never listened to you."

Gary in shock replied. "You wanted to do it too. It's old man Woody! What are we going to do?"

Tommy cried out: "Run! I'll be right behind you!"

Ironically, old man Woody had cut them off at the pass. "Now hold on boys!" He said.

Whispers in the Willows

Tommy and Gary looked at one another in horror. "Please! Please!" Gary pleaded. "Don't make us part of your 'pet cemetery.'"

For some strange reason, Woody found the humor in their state of horror. He laughed like he never laughed before. "Is that what you think of me?"

With a quivering lip and stuttering to answer, Tommy yelped: "Yes, sir!"

"Well, don't you two worry." Woody assured them. "I am not going to hurt you. At least not today."

"You're not?" They said in unison.

"No!" Woody said smiling. "I only do that during a full-moon. You boys still have a week before that happens."

Regardless of how bad they wanted to run for the hills, they knew they couldn't. There was nothing but flat lands before them. Besides, they noticed something about Woody that no one ever discussed. He had a sense of humor.

"I am sorry, boys." Woody said. "But you two are getting ready to position your shovels and plot out land that I consider sacred. I can't let you do that. But if you want to help me, there is something you can do."

With his eyes protruding from his skull, Gary had to ask: "What sir?" Followed by: "Is it run?"

"No, no, no! I am afraid it isn't." Woody said. "If I am correct, you boys will be driving soon."

"Yes!" Tommy was not sure if you answered the question or posed doubt as to whether he would make it to his next birthday.

"Well, then, follow me." Woody said.

Like a bee is drawn to honey, the two boys were for some strange reason were drawn to Woody. They followed him like a sheep follows its shepherd. Woody walked to an old car that had been sitting in his driveway for decades. He pointed to it as it sat dormant. It had every type of dent and ding in it a person could possibly imagine.

"Now." Woody went on to explain. "This old timer has been sitting here for I do not know how many years. In her day, she was a beauty. But I am getting tired of seeing her in my drive. If you want something to do, you two can restore her to her original beauty."

Poor Gary. When it came to common sense, he apparently was not in line when God was handing it out. "You mean, you are not going to kill us?"

Whispers in the Willows

"That's enough with that, please." Woody said. "Here is the deal. I will give you young men whatever it costs to bring this car back to life. And when you complete the project I just asked of you, I will give you the car as a gift."

"No way!" Tommy shouted with enthusiasm. "You are not pulling our legs are you?"

"No, son, I am not. I make this offer to you both on two conditions."

"What's that?" Gary just had to know.

"That's a fair question. First, you two stay away from what I consider sacred ground." Woody explained.

"And the second condition? Sir?" Tommy inquired.

"You complete what you started. If you don't, then I may have to add a cross or two to the 'pet cemetery.' Woody said chuckling.

Chapter 14
"An Invitation to Dinner"

Marilyn scribbled a message on a piece of paper and like a stealth bomber, she quietly flew to Woody's mailbox and stuck an invitation in for dinner.

She knew that Woody was prone to check his mail in the afternoon. She prayed that afternoon would be one such day. As fate would have it, Woody, like an old grandfather clock that chimes on time every morning, noon, and evening, exited the darkened doors from his house. He stumbled over the stones and brush that now covered a sidewalk once paved with brick.

He went to his mailbox where he found a single piece of paper. Initially, he believed it to be a hoax by a townsperson. It was not unusual for people to play pranks on him. He was prone to it. However, there was something quite distinctive and different about this note. Sure it did not have a return address or even a stamp. What it did have was penmanship unparalleled to what he was accustomed to. But it had something else that drew Woody's attention. His name: Woody!

His hands shook terribly as he unfolded the contents of the message that hid behind its covers. It was a personal invitation to dinner. It read: "Woody, we would be honored to have you over for dinner tonight at 6:00 p.m. Charlie's mom."

Whispers in the Willows

Woody did not know what to make of the invitation. Was it some sort of cruel joke? What he could recall of the evening prior, Charlie's father made verbal threats to stay away from he and his family. The thought, though, brought hope to Woody's heart. For someone to honestly take the time to invite him for dinner meant the world.

It had been years since he had socialized with people. He stood there as a statue stands in a garden. He was frozen in time. His eyes started to twinkle. They started to tear. He looked out across the yard only to see Marilyn and Charlie backing out of their driveway.

His fears were quieted when Marilyn made a kind gesture towards him. She stopped the car before putting it in drive: looked at Woody: and clasped her hands as if in prayer. He could faintly see her lips mutter the words "Please come."

Woody acknowledged her invitation. He nodded his head as to affirm her invitation. He then went about his business to cross the jungle that now occupied the sidewalk that was once covered by brick.

Entering his house, a wealth of emotions struck Woody. He could not describe what overwhelmed him more: the meeting he had with Charlie the night before; the threats made by Charlie's father; or the kindness shown by Charlie's mom? He wasn't sure. But this one thing he did know. He did not know what to do.

He proceeded to enter his abode. He walked into what was once considered the bathroom. He used the sleeve from his tattered and torn shirt to wipe away the accumulation of dirt that settled upon its surface over the years. He was horrified by the image that stared back at him.

"That can't be me?" He thought. He reached for the beard that now covered half of his front body. He tugged on it. If the image in the mirror was deceiving, it was affirmed as he could feel his hair dangling with his hand. He then reached behind his head. Again, he was startled to discover the hair on the back of his head was just as long.

He chuckled. "Oh my!" If I am going to accept their dinner invitation, I better try to make myself look presentable. He removed himself from the room where he experienced a rude awakening, and started rummaging through the debris plastered throughout his house. "Where are those blasted scissors?" He said in frustration.

Thankfully, Woody failed to examine the condition of his mouth and teeth. That, however, would come at another time and for another day. In the meantime, Marilyn's invitation rekindled something that had died within Woody a long time ago: it was a fresh look on life.

Chapter 15
"A Table for Four"

Mrs. Orr spent the better part of the day driving the back roads with Charlotte. She wanted to get a feel for the lay of the land. And that's all the eye could see, nothing but land: flat and barren land. While it was beautiful country, it was melancholy. "Funny how one can find beauty in sadness." She thought to herself.

On their drive, Marilyn and Charlotte drove through the Homme Dam Recreation Area hoping to catch Andrew out and about. No luck though. Making their way back home, Marilyn and Charlotte poked about downtown. There was not much to see. They made small talk with some women in the little grocery store. The ladies told Marilyn that a group of moms often got together on the playground of the elementary school for play dates. School was out for the summer but the building was open while the maintenance workers spiffed up the floors and conducted routine inspections.

Upon returning home, Marilyn got busy. Charlotte helped her set up a picnic table on the large inviting porch. Marilyn cooked and Charlotte went off to pick flowers.

"WOW! What's all this?" Andrew said coming up the walkway. "Did my girls do all of this for me?"

"Hi Daddy!" Charlotte squealed running to greet him.

"Hi Charlie!" He replied lifting her up into the air.

"I helped Mommy. Isn't it beautiful Daddy?"

"Yes it is! Did you help Mommy pick those flowers?"

"Yep." Charlotte beamed.

The aroma hit him the moment he stepped into the house. "Boy something sure smells good."

"Hi Honey," Marilyn said giving Andrew a hug. "How did your day go?"

"It was a good day. I am going to shower and change and I'll be down for dinner."

Marilyn grabbed Andrew by the hand before he could exit the kitchen. "You are going to be upset with me, and I'm sorry. I really thought long and hard before I did it." Marilyn pulled Andrew out onto the porch.

"Look what you have been blessed with." Andrew took a long hard look at Marilyn. He was confused and had no idea what she was talking about. Sensing his confusion, "Andy, look at this house. Look at our yard. And look at this setting." Andy looked at the table. A table set with four settings. A lavender tablecloth blew in the breeze. The scent of flowers filled the air. Mason jars

Whispers in the Willows

full of flowers were sitting all over the porch. On the table were a bundle of wildflowers tied with ribbons. Candles glowed adding to the ambiance of the stage set before him.

Marilyn wrapped her arms around Andrew, "Please don't be mad. I invited Woodrow to dinner." Before he could speak, Charlotte bolted out the door with a fist full of papers.

"Daddy, do you want to see the picture I made for Mr. Woody? Don't worry Daddy, I have one for you too!"

Andrew looked at his wife. She stared back with a pleading look. He looked down into Charlotte's excited face. He felt betrayed.

Chapter 16
"So Woody?"

Woody spent the better part of the afternoon grooming. He trimmed his beard; cut his hair, and tried to make himself look presentable. It had been a long time since someone invited him over for dinner. He was still a little skeptical about the invitation. So much so, that he thought on more than one occasion not to attend.

Six o'clock rolled around quicker than he imagined. He started to make his way to the front door when he had this funny feeling. Something just did not seem right. There had to be an ulterior motive. "What would prompt complete strangers to invite him over for supper?" He thought.

For years, he lived in complete isolation. No one ever paid much attention to his welfare. And when people did, it was of a derogatory nature. What was once a skip in his step became a stone wrapped around his ankle. Woody panicked at all the different possibilities: unfortunately his thoughts went back to the threat from the previous night.

As much as he wanted to interact with his new neighbors, fear proceeded to halt his progress. He quietly closed his front door. "No!" He argued. "This must be a set up. Who in their right mind would ever want to get to know me?"

Whispers in the Willows

His line of reasoning continued to follow. He thought about his past. His mind vividly remembered how the people of this small town gave up on him: especially in light of the tragic events that happened that fateful night.

"I can't!" His spirit cried. "Why now?" He thought. But there was a part of him that so desperately wanted to go. "It's been too long. I can't keep living in seclusion." The battle waged as the two opposing thoughts continued to rage from within.

Several minutes elapsed. He would soon have his answer as what to do and how to do it when he heard a gentle knock on his front door. "That's strange." He mumbled. It had been years since anyone took the time to knock on his door. The only time he heard that strange sound was when high school students pulled pranks. It was not unusual for someone to knock on his door in the middle of the night only to disappear behind the bushes. Often times, he could hear the laughter of those pulling such a stunt.

This was different. It was still light outside and he was very much visible to those standing on the porch. He peeked through the door's window. Ironically, a person could not be found. He had enough. He started to turn away from the door only to hear the faint sound of someone tapping on its surface once again. Still, he could not see anyone standing in front of the door.

"No more." He said in disgust. But the soft tapping on the door became more persistent and pronounced. Woody had no choice but to open it. He looked straight ahead only to see nothing. "I must be losing my mind." He thought. As he was about to close the wooden structure that permitted a person to enter or exit, he heard a small voice call out to him. It was Charlie.

"Woody, aren't you coming over for dinner?" Charlie petitioned. "My mommy wanted me to tell you that we are waiting for you and dinner is starting to get cold."

In her little hands were some of the flowers she picked earlier that day. Her presence brought a smile to Woody. How could he ever resist her innocent invitation He looked into her eyes as well as other personal features?

"Now, Miss Charlie." He said. "How could I say 'no' to such a request?"

"I am glad." She said smiling. "I would have missed you if you did not show up."

"Let me get my hat and you can walk me to your house." Woody grabbed a wide brim leather hat and placed it atop his head. He took little Charlie by the hand as they made their way to the dinner waiting them.

It did not take Andrew long to notice a distinct difference about Woody. His beard was cut and neatly groomed and his hair lost several inches that day. Compared

Whispers in the Willows

to their first encounter, Woody almost looked like a civilized human being rather than a cooped up hermit living in a house that some considered a hazard.

Charlie showed Woody to his seat. She made sure it was next to her little table setting. Out of respect, Woody took his hat off before sitting at the table. He made sure he sat after Marilyn and Charlie took their positions at the table.

Andrew was already sitting at the head of the table prepared. His statement was clear. He was the king of his domain. The meal Marilyn and Charlie had specially prepared was something Woody had not seen or smelled in years. The aroma excited and activated his salivary glands.

It was apparent Woody appreciated the time they took to make him feel welcomed in his own neighborhood. Andrew sat at the opposite end of the table from Woody. He struggled to be cordial and to rectify the wrongs of the evening prior.

He blessed the food sitting before them and gave thanks for Woody's presence. As was customary in the Orr household, guests were given the right to fill their plates first. There was so much food that Woody was not sure where to begin. It had been a long time since he had seen such a spread. He had a problem deciding what to put on his plate. For the last several decades, his dinner amounted to nothing more than what the land had to provide.

But now, the dishes of food that covered the table were more than Woody was accustomed too. It did not, however, take Woody long to figure out how to work his fingers around the various dishes, Andrew wanted, no Andrew needed to know a little more about Woody.

He did not hesitant to start a conversation with his line of questioning either. "So Woody." Andrew started. "Today I heard the town owes much to you for contributing to our community." He then went on to add that since they were much younger, they were not sure or specific as to your involvement. "What happened for you to stop with the town's progress?"

Woody took a bite of chicken that covered a large portion of his plate. He answered with silence. It was a road that led to nothing more than a dead end. Therefore, in Woody's mind, it was something he believed did not require an answer. Instead, he found his attention drawn to Charlie. Everything about Charlie disrupted Woody's attention from answering any of Andrew's questions.

It was her eyes, the complexion of her face coupled with the color of her hair. He looked across the table and started his own discussion with her. His attentiveness drew more alarm to Andrew's apprehensions rather than dismiss them.

Whispers in the Willows

Woody proceeded to reach across the table and assisted Charlie with cutting some of the contents on her plate into pieces more manageable for her to chew. Had anyone guessed, he or she would have thought Woody had some experience with children. What they did not know at the time was that he just answered Andrew's question.

Andrew made another stab to start a conversation with Woody. "So," he went on to say, "I see that you have a vehicle sitting in the drive."

"You would be correct." Woody affirmed.

"I cannot help but notice that it has not been driven in years. I know rust has come to inhabit much of the vehicle's surface." Andrew then opened up a wound that he never knew existed. Based on the banged up condition in the front and some dents on the passenger side door, I would guess it was somehow related to a serious car accident."

"You would be correct again." Marilyn noticed that Woody became increasingly uncomfortable by her husband's meager attempt to get to know this strange man that lived next door. Trying to sooth both Andrew's apprehension and Woody's already growing anxieties, Marilyn interjected.

"Woody, my husband is just trying to get a better understanding of you." She said apologetically. "You do not have to answer any question asked: that is, if you don't want to."

She even went so far as to compliment Woody on his appearance. His beard was neatly brushed and trimmed. His hair was no longer dangling uncontrollably. It was cleaned and cut. Marilyn could not help but notice that Woody took time to prepare himself for the meal prepared for him.

Relieved, Woody appreciated Marilyn's assistance. Unfortunately, there were some things puzzling Marilyn. First things first. "Last night, Charlie informed me that you knew her name before you asked for it. How? How did you know her name was Charlie?"

Not wanting to reveal the truth, Woody retorted by reminding Marilyn and Andrew how he heard them speaking to Charlie when they started to unload the truck. Woody's answer was sufficient, at least for that moment.

Like Andrew though, there were some things that were not so much a cause for alarm, but were some things conceived out of curiosity. "Woody." She asked. "I have noticed the crosses that bear the mark for something and of something. 'What? If I may ask?'"

Again, Woody diverted his attention to Charlie. "So young lady, how old are you? If I were not a betting man, I would guess you are four years old soon to turn five."

Whispers in the Willows

Charlie's eyes lit up. "How did you know?" She was surprised. First he knew her name and now her age. It was a question that everyone around the table wanted to know: they wished to know.

After finishing his meal with the Orr's, Woody excused himself from the table. He thanked them for a wonderful dinner, and remarkably, the time he spent with them.

Before leaving Andrew and Marilyn's, Woody removed his wide-brim hat from the hook from which it hung. He went so far at tipping it toward Marilyn before leaving, placed it on top of its desired target, shook Andrew's hand, and ended the evening by bending over to give Charlie a hug and a kiss on her cheek.

Like a gentleman, he personally thanked the family for the invitation to dinner. He exited the gate from which he entered. Andrew and Marilyn thought for sure they heard Woody whistle as he crossed that short stretch of land that separated his place from theirs

Chapter 17
"Walking Behind Weeping Woody's"

Andrew and Charlotte helped Marilyn clean up after dinner. "I'm going for a walk," Andrew stated as he put away the last dish.

"Would you like some company on your walk?" Marilyn asked.

"No thanks." He replied and then walked out the back door.

"I forgot to give Mr. Woody his picture. Can I take it over to him?" Charlotte asked her mother.

"Let's make it a mommy and daughter project."

Together they slipped through the broken fence and cut across Woody's back yard. Tommy and Gary were busy reinventing Woody's rust bucket of a car. Marilyn heard both the boys and her husband talk about the crosses, but this was the first that Marilyn had actually seen them. She was taken by surprise at how nice the backyard was compared to the state of his front yard.

There was a potting table lined with mason jars. By estimation, Marilyn figured there were at least over a hundred of them sitting on the table. Marilyn's mind started to put things together. She thought about the

Whispers in the Willows

mason jar with the photograph coupled with the $5,000 it contained. "I need to give him back that money." Marilyn thought to herself. "Andrew will have a fit if he finds out."

Lost in thought, Marilyn wondered if the crosses were markers indicating spots where mason jars rested beneath the soil. Did the jars contain money? Did the jars contain riches? She did not know. What Marilyn suspected was that the jars contained treasures from Woodrow's past.

"Ready Mommy?" Charlotte's squeaky little voice interrupted her thoughts.

"You already gave Mr. Woody his picture?"

"Yep. And he said he loved it. But then he started to cry."

"He cried?" Marilyn questioned.

"Yep. He said I made him very happy. Why would he cry if he was happy Mommy?"

Taking Charlotte by the hand, Marilyn meandered her way across Woodrow's property. His property seemed to go on forever. "It must have been exquisite at one time." The back of Woody's property had ponds that were now covered with algae, fountains that once gurgled water. There were benches situated in front of areas that used to flaunt nature at her finest.

An arbor of fruit trees led to a gazebo. The gazebo overlooked a dried up riverbed. Marilyn stood speechless.

Off in the distance Marilyn heard Andrew calling for her and Charlie. "We better get going Charlie. We'll come back another day and see if Woodrow will give us a tour." Marilyn could only imagine how beautiful the inside of Woody's house must have been. She could tell that at one time, the place was home to a wealthy family.

"Where ya been?" Andrew asked as Marilyn and Charlotte slipped back through the fence.

"We went on a walk of our own." Marilyn shot back, still reeling from Andrew's snappish attitude.

Andrew retreated to the den. Marilyn tidied up the second floor while Charlotte played in the bathtub. Afterwards, Charlotte skedaddled down the stairs to kiss her dad goodnight. She crawled into his lap to help him finish off the last few crumbs of his apple pie. "I love you Charlie. Sleep tight." Andrew hugged his daughter then gave her a playful swat with the newspaper and told her to scram.

Charlotte said her prayers and then crawled into bed. Marilyn listened while Charlotte read the bedtime story this evening. Marilyn stayed and cuddled with Charlotte making sure that she was fast asleep. She then went to find Andrew.

Whispers in the Willows

"Come with me, I want to show you something." She said urging Andrew to stand up. "You'll need shoes." She added.

Slipping through the broken fence and into Woody's backyard, Marilyn whispered: "There is something about this place that calls to me, Andrew. I can't explain it."

Marilyn, pulling Andrew along by the arm, "Look at these ornate statues. Look at that fountain over there." She led Andrew through the arbor of fruit trees and into the gazebo. "I think Woody is an eccentric that buried money under all those crosses."

Andrew looked out from the gazebo back towards Woody's house. "Money? What makes you think there is money buried in the ground?"

"I didn't get the chance to tell you, and then when I thought about it again, I didn't want to tell you.."

"Tell me what?" Andrew interrupted. Marilyn said, "Woodrow gave me a jar, a mason jar. His yard was littered with them. Inside the jar was an old photograph of a little girl. There was also a wad of money."

"Money?" Andrew said raising an eyebrow. "How much money?"

"Five thousand dollars." Marilyn answered.

"You expect me to believe that the old man, who lives in that dump, would just hand out jars of money?"

"Andrew, it's true. I think he is a wealthy eccentric. Maybe the girl in the picture is a granddaughter that died or something. And Charlotte is bringing back a memory."

Andrew slid his arm around Marilyn. "It's my turn to show you something." Andrew pointed out a beam on the edge of the gazebo. Carved into the wooden beam were the names Woodrow, Alice, Charlene. Followed by Est. 1939.

"You were here? Is this where you came on your walk?"

"Yes" Andrew admitted. Andrew wrapped his arms protectively around Marilyn. "Marilyn, I think the guy is a little crazy. I just don't want anything to happen to you or Charlie." Choking up, Andrew went on. "What if Charlene is the little girl from the picture he gave you? And he thinks Charlie is Charlene?"

Marilyn didn't know how to respond to her husband's fears. She didn't want to patronize Andrew, but she didn't want to be fearful of the elderly man in the dilapidated house either. The words: *"He's a harmless old man"* kept running through her mind.

Chapter 18
"Weeping Woody: Who Are You?"

There was little known about this old miser and still much to learn. This night, both Andrew and Marilyn did some exploring on their own. In the end, they did not know anymore more about the old-timer then they did before he first walked into their yard.

Back at their farmhouse, Andrew settled in front of the television. Marilyn stepped out onto the front porch. There were two things that caught her attention. The first was a small flicker of light coming from Woody's house. By the looks of it, the light dimly lit what she perceived to be the bathroom. She faintly saw Woody's figure standing in front of something. What it was, she was not for certain.

The second thing that captured her attention was buried deep beneath the pillows on the front porch swing. It was another jar. "It can't be." She thought. Her suspicions got the best of her. She reached down and pulled the jar from the cushions. She twisted the top of the jar open only to find a sketch of a little girl. Again, she was struck between the resemblance of the little girl whose face was penciled on this piece of papyrus and Charlie.

It left her mind wondering. "What are you trying to tell us Woody?" She thought. And as before, a clump of money was tightly wrapped around the photograph contained therein. Instead of $5,000.00, it was $3,000.00. Marilyn had a difficult enough time trying to figure out how to explain the first windfall of money. This was only going to add to her dilemma.

There were more questions than answers for the Orr's, and for the first time since their first encounter with Woody, Andrew and Marilyn stood on neutral ground. They wanted to learn more about this man: no longer were they content with speculations, or rumors. They each needed to know the truth.

Because the following day was a Saturday, Andrew was going to make it a point to do what he desired to do prior. He was going to do some digging on his own. Most libraries contained a dearth of information about small towns. Before he and Marilyn retired for the evening, Andrew explained what he was planning to do. For the second time within a matter of hours, the man that once drew them apart was now drawing them together.

To get a jump-start on his day, Andrew woke up extremely early. Though he knew the library would not be open for a few hours, there were some other things he had to attend too: such as refining some prints for the future projects that were soon to unfold.

Marilyn stayed in bed. "It's too early to get up. Love you Honey." She said as Andrew got dressed and headed down the stairs.

Whispers in the Willows

He went to the office where he went over some drawings; revising the ones that had yet to meet zoning requirements, and rubber-stamping the ones ready to proceed with the town's renewal project. After he finished what chores he needed to complete that morning, he then headed toward the local library.

Not exactly sure where to place his shovel, Andrew politely walked up to the librarian and asked where he might go start digging for records of the town's history. Apologetically, the librarian informed Andrew how the library had lost most of its records during a storm some years ago. Apparently, a bolt of lightning struck the building igniting a fire that could not be contained or controlled.

She could see how the words despair and disappointment were etched across Andrew's forehead. "What exactly are you looking for?" She said. Offering her services, she said: "Maybe I can be of some help to you."

"Well, I am not sure where to begin." Andrew stated. "We moved here a few days…

"Oh!" The librarian said enthusiastically. "You must be Mr. Orr! Welcome to Park River. We have heard much about you."

"Thank you." Andrew tried to finish his train of thought when the librarian instinctively knew the reason for his visit.

"Let me guess." She said and then asked. "You want to know something about your neighbor 'Weeping Woody?'"

"How did you know?" He curiously asked.

"His neighbors before you did the same exact thing. Isn't that odd?" She said.

"And what did they find?" Andrew's apprehensions about Woody started to show.

"Not much, I am sorry to say." She countered. "But there may be someone in town who can give you the answers you seek?"

"Who might that be?" Andrew wanted to know. Andrew really needed to know.

"There is an older gentleman who resides in a nursing facility about twenty miles from here." She explained and then continued. "Urban legend says that he and Woody were the best of friends until…" She paused for a period of time.

Having Andrews's full-undivided attention, he asked: "Until what?"

The librarian wasn't quite sure what to say or how to say it.

Whispers in the Willows

Andrew repeated the same question for a second time. "Until what?"

Trying to dodge the question at hand, the librarian changed the topic of discussion. "So what are your plans in developing a new neighborhood?"

Sensing this was somewhat of a sore topic; Andrew decided to draw a line in the sand. "Well ma'am, I wish I could tell you but then that might ruin the surprise, now wouldn't it?"

Andrew turned and started to make his way toward the exit when the librarian caved in to his inquiry. "If you really need to know, then you must talk to Mr. Miller. He will furnish you with the answers to the questions you seek."

Before pushing the door open to exit, Andrew turned to the librarian and politely said: "Thank you again for your time. That was not so hard now was it?"

Breaking the silence that filled this sanctuary of books, the librarian pleaded: "Please go easy on him. He's my grandfather. I am Woodrow's great niece."

Chapter 19
"Where Might I Find Mr. Miller?"

Andrew followed the County Road until he saw the sign pointing to the Good Samaritan Convalescence Home. He turned off the roadway and followed a long gravel road for about a mile. At the end of the gravel road was a small building with a few cars in the parking lot.

"Home for the Elderly" read a sign on the mailbox. There were a few residents sitting on benches in the yard. The grounds were well manicured and dotted with flowering trees and bushes. A few elderly gentlemen sat at a wooden picnic table playing a game of cards.

Inside the home were a few more residents sitting at a large dining table finishing breakfast. A woman in a nurse's uniform greeted Andrew. "Good morning! What can we do for you today?" she asked.

"I'm looking for Mr. Miller." Andrew replied.

"Is he expecting you?"

"No Ma'am. He does not know me. I am new in town and looking for some information that I believe he can help me with."

"I'm sorry, Mr...?"

"Mr. Orr," Andrew said extending his hand to the nurse.

"I'm sorry Mr. Orr, I can't let you go to Mr. Miller's room without his approval. If you will take a seat in the parlor, I will find him. Can you tell me why it is you want to see him? I'm sure he will ask what your business with him is."

"Just tell him I bought the farm next to Weeping Woody."

The nurse excused herself and went off to summon Mr. Miller.

Chapter 20
"Need Some Help"

Charlotte pushed a stool to her bedroom window. It was the perfect perch for her to see down into Woody's backyard. Charlotte spied on him as he went about his trees picking berries and fruits and putting them in small baskets.

Woody looked up to Charlotte's window. Charlotte pushed her window open as far as she could to get it to budge. "Hi, Mr. Woody!" She shouted from her bedroom window.

Woodrow gave Charlotte a salute. "Morning, Miss Charlie."

"Need some help?"

Woody chuckled to himself. With a toothy grin he smiled back at Charlotte, "Sure, come on over missy."

In a flash Charlotte threw on play clothes and jumped on her mom's bed. "Can I go help Mr. Woody pick berries from his trees? Pleeeeze?" She begged.

"Sure honey, just don't go in his house. You need to be in the yard where I can see you."

Whispers in the Willows

Charlotte flew through the broken fence eager to help Woodrow with his fruit collection. Woody handed Charlotte a basket. Charlotte held the basket. Woody loaded it with fresh fruits and berries.

"What are you going to do with all this fruit Mr. Woody?" Charlotte asked.

"I was going to leave it on your porch for your mother. Do you like strawberries, Charlie?"

"My favorite!" Charlotte replied. Woody and Charlotte spent the next fifteen minutes moving from bush to bush, and from plant to plant. Woody loaded the basket with strawberries, red raspberries, and a few pears from his pear tree.

Over at the farmhouse, Marilyn stood hidden behind Charlotte's curtain. She watched the interaction of the two below – and she listened.

"Mr. Woody?"

"Yes Charlie"

"Why is your house so broken?"

"Oh Charlie, broken it is. Yes, my house has been broken for a good long time Little One."

"Hey Mr. Eliott, got you some fresh eggs and cheese from the deli!" Tommy yelled out as he wheeled his bicycle through Woody's side yard. "I came over to finish painting up the fence for Mrs. Orr."

With his long skeleton like fingers, Woodrow reached out and patted Tommy on the back. "You're a fine young man Tommy. Yes sir, a fine young man." Tommy handed the cheese and the carton of eggs to Woodrow.

"Charlie, would you care to assist me in the kitchen?" Woody asked.

"I'm not allowed inside Mr. Woody. I have to stay where my mommy can see me."

Woody thanked Charlotte for helping him with the fruit picking. He divided up the fruit between Charlotte and Tommy and kept some for himself. "I'll be getting on to my chores. You kids behave." And Woody disappeared into his house.

"I have a sister just a little bit older than you Charlotte. You want me to bring her when I come tomorrow? She's always looking for someone to play with." Charlotte was thrilled at the thought of a playmate coming over and ran home to ask her mom.

Chapter 21
"A Wife and Daughter Whisked Away"

Andrew sat on the edge of a chair impatiently watching the clock. He had been waiting for nearly fifteen minutes and was getting ready to leave.

"Oh dear! Oh dear! Oh dear! He wants to see me?" Andrew heard a man's voice saying repetitively.

Andrew stood up and walked towards the reception desk. The nurse was assisting a frail elderly gentleman. "Please have a seat Mr. Orr, I will escort Mr. Miller to a seat in the parlor. You can speak with him there."

Andrew returned to the parlor watching as the nurse guided Mr. Miller to a seat by the window. "Mr. Miller, this is the gentleman I told you about. I would like you to meet Andrew Orr. He bought the farm next to Woodrow Eliott. He would like to talk to you about Woodrow."

"Good old Woody." Mr. Miller said. "Known him all my life. We were best friends. Met in Park River Elementary a long time ago." Tears welled up in Mr. Miller's eyes. We married sisters. He married Alice. I married her older sister Eileen. We stood up for each other in the church. We were best friends."

Mr. Miller paused to collect himself. "Then the war came. We got called up. Sent us to Germany. One day Woody got himself a letter from Alice. She was having a baby. Old Woody was sad and weepy. He wanted to be stateside when Alice had the baby. Platoon started calling him Weeping Woody because he cried for Alice all the time."

"The next letter came and said a baby girl was born. Alice done gone named her Charlene. Woody got a leave and was set to get home to meet his baby girl but came down with the measles. Course he couldn't fly home with the measles. He missed his leave and when he got out of the hospital from the measles, he went back to the war."

Mr. Miller dabbed at his eyes. Andrew listened wide-eyed. He felt deep sadness for Woody.

"By the time Woody got home to Alice, that baby was almost four years old. He was a sap with that baby girl of his. Said he wept for joy every day over that Charlene. He came into some money when he got back from the war on account his folks had passed and left him well to do. So he bought up a bunch of land and built a castle for his princess and lined the road with weeping willows. Said he wept tears of sadness and tears of joy. He found beauty in a good weeping."

Mr. Miller stared out the window. He was silent for several minutes. "Mr. Miller?" Andrew inquired.

"Well, one night Alice and the baby come over to see Eileen. A bad storm blew in from the west. Spawned

Whispers in the Willows

a tornado in town. There was lots of rain. I mean lots of rain. The lightning was frightening. It hit the library and burnt it to the ground. It was an awful night." Tears rolled down Mr. Miller's face.

"Alice wanted to get home to Woodrow. They were crazy about each other. She said he'd be worried. With all the rain, Alice's car sunk down into the mud; so I offered to take her and Charlene home."

With tears still streaming down his cheeks, Mr. Miller continued: "We were coming up to the bridge at the river when the river washed up over the banks. The flood wiped out the bridge and my car went down the river with the bridge. I panicked, Alice and the baby were screaming. Next thing I knew, we washed up on a shore. Alice had drowned. Charlene's body was never found. The car was found down river with a tree lying across it. Flattened the car to a pancake."

"Heartbreaking." Andrew said and joined in the orchestra of tears. "I never forgave myself. Had I insisted Alice stay over, she wouldn't have died that night. My good buddy Woodrow reached out to me and I couldn't even face him."

"I left town. I left Eileen. I moved away and didn't come back. I was filled with grief and guilt. I heard through the grapevine that Woodrow didn't blame me. But I was afraid to see him. He retreated into the castle he built for Alice and his princess and became a recluse. He planted more weeping willows. Woody's heart stopped beating the moment Alice and Charlene were whisked away."

"As he grew older, people made up wild stories about him. Young kids messed with him. They broke out his windows. Vandalized his property. He let it go. I came back to town about thirty years after that dreadful night. Went to visit Woodrow. We laughed, we cried. I felt exonerated. The burden I carried was no longer. Woodrow and I, we fished, we worked in his yard and gardens. But his sadness was still there. He never got over his Alice and his baby girl."

The nurse interrupted, "I think Mr. Miller is getting tired and we should cut the visit short." She helped Mr. Miller to his feet and led him back towards the stairs. "If you see my friend Woodrow, tell him to come visit this old man."

Chapter 22
"Charlie, Is That You?"

It was an emotional ride home for Andrew. He cried as he thought about everything Mr. Miller had told him. Andrew felt compelled to go to the river. He, of course, didn't know what bridge would have been washed out some fifty years ago, but he made his way to the Park River. He stood on the banks and wept for Alice and Charlene. He wept for Mr.Miller and Woody. And he wept out of shame for the way he treated Marilyn.

Andrew looked across the bridge as it spanned the river. He walked toward its base and sat along the river's bank. He could hear the mighty rushing water as it raced downstream. He closed his eyes and envisioned the accident of that terrible night so long ago. He could not even imagine the fear that filled the hearts of those in the vehicle. Even more frightful was the thought of losing everything and almost everyone a person ever loved.

He started weeping for Woody. "Oh! Stop it!" He thought. "People will start talking about you!" He laughed at the thought. His time of reflection and remorse was suddenly snapped when a branch from a tree down river broke and fell into the river. Andrew opened his eyes only to be startled by what he saw. He was not sure if the tears had blurred his vision or if, by chance, he was dreaming. He wiped his eyes dry and there it stood standing.

Of all the trees that stuck out from the rest, it was this one. In fact, it was the only one of its kind among the plant life and vegetation along this long stretch of rushing water. It was a Weeping Willow. "How odd?" Andrew said aloud. His interest peeked as this tree stood tall and proud. Something literally pulled Andrew to the place where this Weeping Willow planted its roots.

He found himself walking along a path that had long since been hidden for decades. He could tell by the brush that someone else also had recently fought his or her way through the brushes and weeds that blanketed the path. Like the adventurers of past, Andrew was compelled to continue his exploration for new land, new discoveries, and new answers.

It was difficult for Andrew to walk along the fast moving stream as he tried to keep pace with the flow of water. Several times he lost his balance almost sending him off the deep end: physically and emotionally. He so desperately tried to picture everything that transpired. He felt himself moving back in time.

Looking back toward the bridge, Andrew could see the car lose control as it attempted to cross. He could see the front of it taking a nosedive into a river that showed no mercy for anything or anyone who dared to enter its depths. He could hear the screams for help from those trapped in the car. He heard the prayers of each person as they pleaded for forgiveness, mercy, and salvation.

Whispers in the Willows

Then from out of nowhere, his mind locked on little Charlene. Her cries for her mommy ripped a hole in his heart. He could view the horror on her little face as she would soon become one with the river. He saw Alice fighting so hard to stay alive so that she could tend to her daughter's screams. But that was not meant to be. The currents were too strong.

Alice's concerns for Charlene sent chills down Andrew's spine. To know that it was she who gave life to her little girl only to have it swept away down stream. Alice's feelings of hopelessness and helplessness were too much. He could never fathom the horrors Alice must have felt as she too took her final breath.

"Woody!" He screamed. Having a wife and daughter of his own, Andrew came to a full understanding of how time could literally stop for someone. How someone's desire to live ceases. Andrew fell to his knees. He looked unto the clear blue skies. Just as Alice and Charlotte pleaded for their lives that fateful night, Andrew made his own pleas. It was there that Andrew sought forgiveness for his actions toward a man who lost everything so precious in life.

As he clasped his hands together in prayer, a gentle wind pushed him along. His journey was far from being over. Having walked what seemed to be an eternity, Andrew finally made it to the place that beckoned him. It was the Weeping Willow tree.

At the base of it roots, Andrew found a memorial marker with pictures of both Alice and Charlene. Andrew noticed that someone had recently placed a fresh bouquet of flowers in front of it. If he was not mistaken, the flowers, in some fashion and form, resembled those found in Woody's backyard. They seemed to resuscitate life to those who perished. "It can't be!" Andrew mumbled. "He is too old and this is too far for him to walk."

His eyes moved from the flowers to the pictures. He became even more remorseful when he again noticed the striking resemblance between Woody's little girl and his little girl. But there was something else that caught Andrew off guard. Both girls shared the same birth dates. The only difference between the two was the years separating them: fifty to be exact.

Andrew knelt down. He started to rub his fingers across both pictures. He made a vow to do everything he could to help restore hope for what time Woody had remaining. He also made a mental note to see how those flowers found their place that now lay before Alice and Charlene's marker.

Trying not to disturb the dead, Andrew lifted himself from this sacred ground where he knelt, and, with the utmost respect and reverence walked back to his car. Every now and then he heard something rustle amongst the leaves. For a moment or two, he thought he was

Whispers in the Willows

being watched and followed. "It's your imagination playing tricks on you." He tried to reason. "Or is it?"

Ironically, and without any explanation, the sounds ceased when Andrew made it back to his car. He looked out his driver side window. The hair on the back of his neck stood on end when he thought he witnessed something inanimate scurrying through the foliage. He so desired to remove himself from his vehicle, but again rationalized that it was all a figment of his imagination.

He started the ignition to his car and headed for home. Before crossing the bridge, he slowed down to look toward the Weeping Willow tree. He suddenly stopped his car when he saw what he believed to a little girl standing along the river's edge. "Charley? Is that you?" The little girls figure soon vanished.

Chapter 23
"I Owe You an Apology"

With a change of heart, Andrew headed home. He was eager to get home and share with Marilyn, the conversation he had with Mr. Miller. He was eager to share his change of heart, and he was eager to have a real conversation with Woody.

"Hi boys." Andrew waved his arm out the window as Tommy pedaled towards him. Andrew stopped in the middle of the dead end road that led to his house. "Working for Woody today?" He queried.

"Yeah," Tommy replied. "I finished painting the fence and then cleared that old junker sitting in Woody's drive way. He said if me and Gary fixed it up we could have it."

"Wow! Andrew said sticking a high five out the window. "Be careful riding home."

"I will Mr. Orr."

In his rearview mirror, Andrew watched Tommy ride out of sight. With his focus back to the road in front of him, Andrew surveyed the panorama before his eyes. The symbolism of the Weeping Willows was powerful. As a person who worked to maintain the integrity of the land and natural resources, Andrew knew the impact

Whispers in the Willows

those Weeping Willows were meant to signify. The drooping branches looked like tears falling from the sky.

Andrew pulled into the driveway. He wiped tears from the corners of his eyes. "Hi Charlie, how's my girl?" Andrew said walking over to the sandbox where Charlie was sitting. "What are you making kiddo?"

"Pie, Daddy. Want a piece?"

"Pie? Sure, I'd love a piece." He said pretending to take a bite of Charlie's sand pie.

"What have you been up to today besides making pies?"

"Well, Charlie said, I helped Mr. Woody pick stuff from his bushes. Then Tommy came over and I helped him paint the fence. Then Mommy took the berries from Mr. Woody's yard and made them into pies!" Charlotte was excited as she shared her day with her dad.

"Tell Daddy about the car." Marilyn said sticking her head out the window.

"Tommy pulled the weeds off Mr. Woody's car and me, and mommy, and Tommy, and Mr. Woody sat in the old car and ate pie. It was great daddy. I even got to be the driver."

"Sounds like a great day Charlie." Andrew said as he tussled Charlotte's hair and headed in the house.

"Sit down Marilyn. Boy have I got a story for you."

Marilyn and Andrew sat at the kitchen table. He took hold of her hands and relayed the story Mr. Miller told him earlier in the day. He then shared with her about his stop at the river.

"Her body was never recovered Marilyn." He said about Charlene. "Her remains rest somewhere on the bank of that river. If I can find out where the car went into the river Marilyn, I can trace the flow and the curvature of the river and maybe figure out where that little girl surfaced."

Marilyn sat quietly taking it all in. "I know you are going to think I'm crazy." Andrew continued. "I swear I saw Charlene running along the river bank."

"What?" Marilyn gasped.

"You know how you just get that feeling?" Andrew went on. "I think there is something there. We need to find her Marilyn. We need to reunite Woody with *his* Charley.

"I owe Woody an apology. I'm going to go see him after dinner." Squeezing Marilyn's hands, Andrew became choked up. "I owe you and Charlie an apology." Andrew stood and pulled Marilyn to him. "I should have known better. Your intuition has never led you in the wrong direction. I'm sorry I doubted you. You're a beautiful person Marilyn. I love you because you are a trusting soul and see the best in everybody; including me."

"Oh Andrew." Marilyn embraced her husband and shared a passionate kiss. She whispered in his ear. "I've missed you sweetheart."

Chapter 24
"Where to Begin?"

After dinner Andrew headed over to Woody's house. He saw a flickering light shining through the planks that covered a boarded up window. "Hmmmm, I should fix these steps for the old man," Andrew thought as he walked cautiously among the rotted boards on Woody's back porch.

He rapped on the door, but Woody did not come. He pounded a little more vigorously. "Woody!" He shouted. Still nothing. Andrew jiggled the doorknob and the door swung open. Andrew pushed the door open a bit wider and stuck his head in.

The acrid smell immediately overtook him. He took a step back into the fresh air and gagged. Holding his breath, he pushed the door open and stepped into Woody's kitchen. He was sickened by what he saw. The counter tops were littered with plates of left over food scraps. Dishes were piled on the table. Flies and maggots were crawling on every horizontal surface in the kitchen. Large buckets with brown water lined the wall by the back door. Peeling paint and loose plaster lay on the floor. Most of the wooden floor was extremely soft and saggy. It appeared as though it wouldn't support much weight. The place was revolting.

Whispers in the Willows

Andrew withdrew and headed back to the farmhouse. Hitting the shower, he tried to wash the filth he felt crawling on him. "How can anyone live like that?" He asked in disbelief.

"We have to do something Andrew."

"Marilyn, Woody needs so much help I don't even know where to begin. But I have an idea."

"What is that?" Marilyn asked. She was elated and excited to see Andrew's enthusiasm to reach out to Woody. Whatever happened at the bridge that afternoon definitely altered Andrew's attitude and course of action he was soon to embark upon.

"The first thing I have to do is find Woody. He did not answer his door. I have a hunch where I might find him." Andrew explained and then went on to add: "If I could find a map of the river's topography and geography of fifty years ago, coupled with an accurate account of the storm that swept through that evening, then I might be able to calculate where to find his little girl's final resting place."

Marilyn wanted to share in Andrew's enthusiasm. She really did. However all records were destroyed in the fire that consumed the library. Not wanting to sabotage his plans or his participation, Marilyn still had to ask. "Honey, where might you find any type of record detailing and describing everything you just told me?"

Her question was a fair question. It was one that Andrew asked himself. The answer to the mystery was not found buried in the shelves of a library, but rather was sitting right before his very eyes that very day. At the time, Andrew did not realize the significance.

His eyes lit up when he thought about Marilyn's query coupled with the prints from antiquity blanketed by all the blueprints. Excitedly, he yelped: "On my desk! They are on my desk!"

"What are you talking about?" With a puzzled look on her face, Marilyn asked.

"The prints from 50 years ago are on my desk!" Andrew elaborated. "I had an assistant dig them up from the last development that took place. It was fifty years ago."

Proud of his discovery, Andrew went on to explain. "You see, before the developers can begin shuffling dirt from one place to the next, I have to survey the surrounding properties to make sure there were no significant changes to the landscape. The answer is at my office snuggly resting on my desk."

His enthusiasm was contagious. Believing her husband had struck gold; Marilyn took Andrew by the hands and posed one simple question. "Well?"

"Well, what?" Andrew asked.

Whispers in the Willows

"Well," Marilyn said. "Are you going to stand here all night or are you going to disturb those prints sleeping on your desk?"

Andrew was somewhat shocked, but not surprised by Marilyn's statement. "Are you sure? I can pick them up in the morning."

"You go, honey!" Marilyn ordered. "Woody has wept for fifty years. I would hate to see him weep another day. And besides, I promised the ladies at the church to help set up for next week's Vacation Bible School. I will take Charlie with me. It will give her a chance to meet some other children.

Chapter 25
"Rainy Day Fund Revived"

The women from the Ladies Guild were at the little church working on props and decorations for Vacation Bible School. Marilyn didn't want to be mislabeled as a town gossip, but she wanted to talk to someone, anyone for that matter, about the night Woodrow's family perished in the flood

"Hello Marilyn, I'm Mrs. Clifford and this is my daughter Sam. My son Tommy sure enjoys riding over to your house and helping Woodrow."

"It's nice to finally meet you Mrs. Clifford." Marilyn said extending her hand.

"Tommy tells me you have a daughter around Sam's age. Sam is going to be seven in the fall."

"Charlotte will be five at the end of the summer. She is out on the playground. Sam, why don't you go introduce yourself? She would love a little playmate."

Sam ran off to find Charlotte. She too was excited at the thought of having a playmate around her age.

Overhearing the conversation between the two women, a woman approached Marilyn. Offering her hand, she introduced herself. "Hello. I'm Cheryl. I run the library.

Whispers in the Willows

I met your husband when he came in looking for town records. Did he manage to make contact with my grandfather?" Cheryl asked.

"He sure did and what a heartbreaking tale your grandfather told."

"Alice was my grandmother's sister. After Alice and Charlene died, my grandfather disappeared. My grandmother was never the same. My mother was only a child at the time. She grew up not knowing her dad."

Cheryl continued: "Woodrow pretty much vanished from the town after that night." Collecting her thoughts as if lost in the past, Cheryl was silent for a moment.

"When the library was hit by fire during that storm so long ago, an anonymous donor gave enough cash for the town to have it restored to its original condition."

"An anonymous donor gave money for the school board to add a playground behind the school. The same amount was given to build a playground here at the church. The money was left at the Mayor's Office inside glass mason jars. Along with the wads of money were notes instructing what was to be done with the it."

"There is a fund at the bank with over $100,000 in it. The fund was started from the money jars that were found stashed all over the town. Whenever the town needs something, or a family needs assistance, cash is taken from the 'Rainy Day Fund.'"

"Many people think Woody is the financial culprit who leaves the money jars."

Marilyn didn't know if she should tell Woody's secret. She decided to stay mum about the jars Woody left in her yard.

"Cheryl, I know someone who desperately needs assistance and would never ask for it. Whom do I talk to about this 'Rainy Day Fund?'"

"The Mayor." Cheryl replied. "He should be stopping by tonight to drop off the cookies his wife baked for the snack tomorrow night."

Marilyn excused herself and took her decorating to the front of the church so that she would not miss the Mayor when he arrived with the cookies.

When his car pulled up, she offered to help him carry in the baked goods and ran her idea by him. "I love it Mrs. Orr. I will assemble a team. I will be in touch."

Marilyn could not wait to get home to tell Andrew about her big revelation.

When he returned with blueprints in hand, Marilyn told him about her conversation with the Mayor.

"He is going to assemble a team to make the summer cottage on the back of Woody's property livable. He assured me they had enough money to run water and electric and make it a place where Woody could live year round." Marilyn went on to tell Andrew about the jars of money and the rainy day fund. Andrew agreed that it was a great idea to fix up the little barn like structure back by Woody's gazebo.

"He doesn't need that big house." Andrew reasoned. "It's much too big for him to take care of. The summer cottage would be perfect for him. Not much upkeep."

"Do you think he will be upset?" Marilyn frowned.

"I don't think so Marilyn. I think he would be content to have a clean and a safe place to live."

"The Mayor said that the town would step in to bring his house to code and with no heirs, he believed that Woody left the property to the town upon his passing."

Chapter 26
"Woody Found Weeping"

Andrew darted out the front door like a little kid getting ready to go to the local ice-cream stand. Racing to his car, he redirected his steps toward Woody's. Woody, he thought, would be a valuable asset is detailing and describing the lay of the land fifty years ago.

His stride led him to land on Woody's front porch. He jumped the steps only to stand before the door he left hours ago. Hoping Woody would this time answer the door and accept the invitation to go on Andrew's quest for new discoveries, Andrew tried his hand again by knocking on Woody's door. But there was no answer. There was no Woody.

"Woody! Where are you?" Andrew wondered. He turned only to see Marilyn and Charlie back out of the driveway and head down the lane. He shook his head. For a moment, he felt like someone burst the air from his balloon.

Standing still, a gentle breeze kicked up again. Andrew could not believe it. He was literally being pulled to his car. He looked down the lane only to notice that all the limbs hanging from the Weeping Willows were motionless. He also noticed how everything around him remained calm. "How strange?" He pondered as he was being drawn to his car.

Whispers in the Willows

He did not have a choice in the matter. He was being driven by something higher than he. He got into the car, sat behind the wheel and started to make his way down the lane. He looked in his rearview mirror and was shocked to see the image reflecting back to him. Yes, it was Woody's house. But there was something remarkably different. For the first time, Andrew could see Woody's place as it looked some fifty years ago.

He jerked his head back in disbelief. "What is going on?" He could not help but think. The surprises continued. Though his hands were at the helm, his car seemed to be on autopilot. Andrew wanted to take the shortest route to his office, but his steering wheel told him different. When he tried to turn right, the car turned left. When he wanted to slow down for a light, the car sped up.

"This is not funny anymore!" He shouted to the heavens. Eventually though, he surrendered to the car's wishes. Remarkably it led him to the bridge he frequented earlier that day. Andrew then realized what was expected of him. Finally he regained control of his vehicle. Once he made it to the other side of the bridge, he parked his car off the side of the road.

He crossed the street and started to retrace his own steps from his first visit. Approaching the Willow Tree that stood tall and firm over the crescent of the riverbanks, Andrew could hear a voice. It was Woody's. Andrew stopped some feet from where Woody stood.

Not to disturb Woody in the moment, Andrew watched, listened, and waited.

There he saw Woody clasping a bouquet of flowers freshly picked from his own back yard. Woody was not so much speaking as he was weeping. Andrew could hear the pain that held Woody's heart. He could feel the pain that held Woody captive for so long.

"I am so, so sorry Alice." Woody cried. "Had I known that evening, I would have told you to stay where you were."

"I miss you sweetheart. I miss my little girl. Every time I take a breath, I can't help but think of yours and Charley's last." He wept bitterly. "It should have been me; not you and Charley." Woody let out a blood-curdling scream. It echoed through the woods, across the river, and toward the bridge from which his wife and child died.

There was a long pause. Andrew wept as Woody wept. Woody removed the flowers that once sat in front of the marker and replaced them with the one's he held so tightly. He started to speak again. "We have some new neighbors." He added. Andrew could see Woody directed his conversation to his little girl Charley.

"They have a little girl that looks exactly like you sweetie. She even has the same nickname as you." To gain whatever ground he lost kneeling, Woody placed

Whispers in the Willows

both hands on the marker. He then took his right index finger only to gently rub the cheek of his little girl. "She reminds me so much of you!"

Trying to remain composed, Woody took a deep breath. However, Woody was never one to hide his emotions. He sobbed as if he just received the news of his family's demise. "They seem to be nice folks." He said in attempt to bring solace to Alice and Charley.

"I am not sure about the husband though. I believe he means well, but hasn't figured it out. He has not figured me out." Woody reflected for another second. "I can't say I have been a saint either…"

Woody's sentence was snapped short when Andrew accidentally stepped on some twigs snapping them into pieces. Woody looked up with tear stained eyes. His hair and beard were waving with the winds that blew against the river's flow.

Andrew's presence did not come as a surprise to Woody. "It's about time you made it." Woody commented.

"How did you know I would be here?" Andrew had to know.

"I just did. I knew in my heart of hearts there was good in you." Woody then looked down toward Alice and Charlene. He introduced his two girls to Andrew. "Alice and Charley, this is Mr. Orr. The man I was telling you about." He laughed. "Something tells me that you have already met him."

Andrew took a step toward Woody. His arms were stretched out as if it to give Woody a hug. Ironically, Woody welcomed those arms coming towards him. He stood up from the place he knelt and reciprocated the gesture. There both men stood embracing one another. There both men stood weeping together.

"I'm sorry Woody." Andrew cried. "I want to help you. But for me to do that I need you to help me."

"How?" Woody said tearfully.

"I need you to come with me. I think I know how to bring closure to your pain." Woody could sense the sincerity in Andrew's words. At that moment, Woody set aside the threats made to him by the man who now held him like a newborn baby.

Woody sobbing in Andrew's shoulders, said: "Thank you. I will do whatever I can do to help fix this hole in my soul."

With that both men proceeded to the car.

Chapter 27
"Where are We Going?"

Andrew and Woody started down the trail leading to the car. Andrew followed Woody's lead until they made it to the car. Andrew stood amazed at how effortlessly Woody walked along the path recently re-opened a few days ago. He could not help but think: "For a man so frail and fragile, he sure moves around well."

What Andrew did know was how Woody was once a real warrior. During the second world war, Woody along with fellow soldiers gained the reputation of walking up to the enemy unnoticed and unscathed. As a result, many lives were spared, as the enemy had no choice but to surrender to the American forces. There are just some things a person never forgets: such as riding a bike, military training, and let's not forget, losing those people who are near and dear to one's heart.

Woody halted his march when he and Andrew got to the car. He looked at Andrew and asked: "Where are we going? I take it you have a place in mind other than back home."

Andrew answered: "You are correct. We are going to my office to survey some old drawings of the land."

"What are you hoping to find?" Woody inquired.

Andrew tried to throw a curve ball at Woody. Hoping that his answer would satisfactorily sooth Woody's inquiry, he said: "Well, Woody, it is has been brought to my attention you are an expert at reading maps and if anyone remembers the lay of this land, it is you."

His best efforts at evading Woody's question were shot down. "You did not answer my question, young man. What are you hoping to find is what I asked?"

Andrew acted as if the he could not hear Woody because of the noise pollution coming from the river's rhythm, the birds chirping in the trees, and the gentle winds that swept across the street. Woody shook his head. What he did next was beyond belief. He stood watch over the driver's side door. He guarded it as if he was protecting the wall of a garrison.

"Woody." Andrew had to ask. "What in the world do you think you are doing?"

"Well friend. You did not answer my question. Therefore, you must want me to trust you. Back in my day, trust had to be earned. It runs both ways, don't you think?"

"I cannot agree with you more." Andrew retorted.

"Then, you are going to earn and learn to trust me." Woody countered. "Now give me the keys to your car."

Whispers in the Willows

"Common Woody. You are not serious?" There was a long pause. Andrew could see the sincerity in Woody's eyes. Sheepishly he asked: "Are you?"

"Hand them over, or I will start walking the highway home." Woody said.

"I'm not going to win this argument, am I?"

"Son, I don't think so." Woody snapped back. "Either give me your keys, or keep whatever you have planned to yourself. It's that plain and simple."

Knowing this was a fight that could not be won, Andrew conceded to Woody's concessions. He reached deep into his front right pocket, disturbed the keys from their sleep, and surrendered them to Woody. He then walked in front of the car and took his position in the passenger seat.

Woody opened the driver's side door and took the wheel. His eyes lit up as he placed the keys in the ignition. "Oh! Like riding a bike." He mumbled. His excitement grew all the more when he could hear the engine purr like a kitten. "Yes!" He shouted.

His elation would soon turn to frustration when he could not find the gearshift that rose from the floorboard of the vehicle. Trying to mask his lack of knowledge, Woody looked around the front of the car to see how he might go about getting it to at least budge.

He jumped out of his seat as he turned the switch to the windshield wipers. "Well, that didn't work." He stuttered. He was startled as he inadvertently turned on the stereo. The music that blared from the speakers made his beard stand on end. Woody grimaced while Andrew grinned and giggled like a little boy.

"What's so funny?" Woody snorted.

"Nothing!" Andrew laughed. "Are you done playing around or are you going to figure out how to get the car out of park? We don't have all day you know."

"Give me one more chance!" Woody echoed. He stared the dashboard over. "I got it!" He said confidently. His hand just happened to glance the handle responsible for putting the car in motion. Andrew drew a deep sigh of relief when Woody accidentally turned on the emergency flashers.

"Oh! Blasted!" He chirped. "Okay! You win. You were willing to trust me to at least try. That's good enough. Here. You drive."

Andrew removed himself from the passenger seat. He looked up to the heavens and said out loud. "Thank you."

"What was that young man?" Woody snickered.

"Nothing Woody." Andrew said smiling. "It was absolutely nothing."

Whispers in the Willows

The men swapped positions. With the car still purring, Andrew placed his right foot on the brake, took hold of the proper mechanism to place the car in motion, and started to drive toward town. He heard Woody mumble to himself: "Dang it. I should have followed my first instincts!"

It was not a very long drive into town or through town. Woody's eyes glistened as he started to remember how things use to be, and was grieved to see that not much had changed either. He started to point out certain landmarks only to give a brief description behind each one. He did smile to see how the city had used its "Rainy Day Fund" to renovate certain aspects of the town. The library brought the most joy to his heart.

Within fifteen minutes of driving, Andrew and Woody made it to the office. It brought back memories Woody had buried for so many years. He stepped out of the car and stared at the old stone structure. Woody recounted the many times, the many steps, and the many hours he spent within its structure.

"Woody." Andrew politely said. "Follow me."

"I'm coming. I'm coming!" Woody whispered. Andrew opened the back door to this historical building. Woody noticed that nothing had really changed since he last lay his feet on its floors. He quietly followed Andrew all the while reminding himself "to trust him." Woody's pursuit came to an end as Andrew drew the keys to unlock office door.

Woody hesitated to walk through the doors. "What's wrong, Woody?" Andrew asked.

"This used to be my office." Woody groaned in grief. Andrew could tell that Woody's mind spiraled through a wind tunnel of time. He knew Woody could not cross that threshold now holding him back.

"Wait right here, Woody." Andrew was starting to prove himself a friend and, in Woody's eyes, a fellow soldier. He went to his desk and started to shuffle through all the prints of past and present. Finally he found the maps from memories past. He snatched the drawings and brought them to Woody.

Woody's mind was still caught between the present and the past. Andrew laid the sketches on a table that rested comfortably in the corridor. He walked up to Woody to redirect his attention to the papers before them. "Woody." Andrew softly said. "I need you to look at these drawings."

From out of nowhere, Woody's mind returned to the present only to be thrown and tossed back to the past. Those were his drawings. He recognized every little detail about the landscape and the things that were supposed to be and never were. He gazed at the maps as if he were a soldier surveying a foreign field.

Whispers in the Willows

He started to talk. He started to explain everything that suddenly came to life. Andrew did not have to ask a question. Woody had answered them all. Woody looked at the river where Alice and Charlene drowned. "This is not right!" Woody yelled out as he looked at the course and the flow of the water that etched the land.

"Woody, what is not right?" Andrew asked.

"The river." Woody said.

"What about the river?"

"It's not the same river." Woody started to weep. "After the accident, local officials thought it best to widen it."

"Is that all?" Andrew begged to know.

Woody could not control his tears. "I pleaded with them not to make the changes right away. I wanted to find my 'Charley.' But they would have nothing to do with it." He sobbed uncontrollably.

Andrew could tell that Woody's pain was just as fresh and deep as the riverbed they know discussed. "Woody?" Andrew said filled with compassion. "What else is different."

Staring at the print, Woody cried. "Charley, I tried. I tried to find you. They wouldn't let me."

"Woody. Please tell me. What is different?" Andrew begged to know.

"Because of the floods, they redirected the river to flow twenty degrees NNW." He said uncontrollably. "The bend starts from the point where I planted the Willow Tree. They also built a dam some miles down the road to help control the rising waters."

His next words were like a sword piercing through Andrew's heart. Andrew felt every fiber of Woody's pain. "If you are looking to find my Charley, please, I beg you…" Woody wept endlessly…"Please find her. I cannot rest until you do."

Going against everything he felt, Andrew approached Woody and held onto this old-time warrior. He now understood how Woody was rendered "Weeping Woody." They say the best form of comfort is silence. Andrew remained silent as Woody sobbed in his shoulder.

Chapter 28
"A New Day Begins"

The following morning Tommy and Gary showed up to the farmhouse and this time they brought friends. Tommy also brought his sister Samantha along. They assembled in the Orr backyard and devised a plan to get the little summer cottage on Woody's property cleared out and cleaned up.

Marilyn removed a section of the fence for easier access to Woody's back property. Andrew helped clear brush to make a path for the tractor. He, along with the help of the boys, then assembled a rudimentary trailer with lumber and spare parts found in the barn.

Tasks were assigned and the work began. Everything in the little cottage was to be removed and then sorted into piles: keep and clean, throw away, or burn.

Fortunately the little cottage was far enough away from Woody's house that he couldn't see the commotion taking place. Charlotte and Sam helped keep him distracted. Woody spent part of the day sitting on the Orr's porch entertaining Charlotte and Sam with stories of "the good days."

The little cottage was sparsely furnished. It didn't take long for the work crew to empty it. The cottage had a small living room, a kitchen with a dining area, a bathroom, and two small bedrooms. There was a nice enclosed screen room off the back and a front porch off the front. The house had working well water, septic, and electricity. All would need to be updated. Mr. Clifford told the Orr's that once the housing developments were approved, the town would run new water, gas, and sewer lines. For the present they would have to continue to use propane, wells, and septic systems.

Surprisingly the cottage was not filthy. It had been closed up for many years and had a musty odor. The furniture was covered with protective blankets and sheets and didn't appear to be in too bad of shape.

Marilyn had the boys take all of the furnishings and store them in her barn. It would be her job to clean the pieces and decide which ones would go back into the cottage and which pieces to toss. "If Woody has not used this stuff in fifty years, he won't miss it now." She surmised.

Later that afternoon, Mr. Clifford and the mayor stopped by the farmhouse. They followed the trail leading back to Woody's summer cottage. "I've made several phone calls this morning." The mayor told Marilyn. "I have volunteers who offered their professional services to conduct the inspections for necessary updates."

Then Mr. Clifford spoke: "I am donating the services of my company to come in and do any remodeling, plaster work, or painting that needs done." The mayor and Mr.

Whispers in the Willows

Clifford poked around the little dwelling making notes on their clipboards.

"It was good to see you again Marilyn."

"Same here Mr. Clifford."

"Please, call me Thomas." He said giving her a quick hug.

"Mrs. Orr, I don't see that it will take a lot to get this place in shape." The mayor said. "We will get started in the next day or two with the inspections and I think we can have the work complete in a week, maybe a little longer if we run into anything major."

"Wow, that would be wonderful!"

Marilyn followed the mayor and Thomas back over to her property and showed them some of the furnishings that were hauled out of the cottage. The mayor offered the services of the town refuse company to haul away the junk. Marilyn expressed her gratitude and then headed to the kitchen to clean up and prepare lunch for her crew of hard workers.

Chapter 29
"Jonah and The Whale"

Andrew helped Marilyn fix lunch. He sat down for a quick bite with Charlotte and her friend Sam and then he was off. Giving Marilyn a hug, he said, "I have a survey team to work with this afternoon. I'll see you at suppertime. Honey you are such a blessing to everyone who knows you. That is a tremendous task you have taken on." He gave her a quick kiss and a playful pat on the rear and headed off to work.

Andrew met his Corp of Engineers at the field office and together they headed for the dam. On the ride out, Andrew told his colleagues the story about Woody and the night of the storm. He choked up as shared the story about Alice and Charlene. He wept as he told them of his initial reaction to Woody and the disgraceful behavior towards Marilyn.

He went on to tell them about the flowers on the riverbank, the old Geological Survey of the river, and Charlene's remains. Andrew's coworkers were fascinated by the story. Like Andrew, they were new to the area. As they spread their tripods, locators, and rods, they hypothesized about the whereabouts of Charlene's missing remains.

After completing their environmental survey, the team headed back to the field office. A few of the guys

Whispers in the Willows

stuck around to look at the earlier river flow maps that Andrew had strewn across his desk. In a huddle, they drew lines, circles, and put X's on the river map.

Andrew rolled the map up, stuck it under his arm and headed home.

Andrew caught sight of the cars in the church parking lot. Remembering that Vacation Bible School was this week, he pulled into the church.

"Hey Preacher Dan." He said giving a firm handshake.

"Ah! Good evening Mr. Orr. Are you here to lend a hand?"

"Excuse me, pastor?" Andrew replied with a puzzled look on his face.

Preacher Dan went on to explain: "The cafeteria ladies didn't show up tonight. The staff really could use some help passing out juice and cookies. You'll be the hit of the evening." Preacher Dan said with a smile.

"Take me to the cookies and I'll be glad to pitch in!"

"Daddy! What are you doing here?" Charlie shouted with excitement.

Marilyn, somewhat shocked to see Andrew standing in the kitchen asked, "Hey honey, what are you doing here?"

"I heard there were cookies."

Marilyn brought her group of preschoolers into the little social hall for their snack. While the children enjoyed the treat, Andrew and Marilyn discussed how to move forward with Woody and the search for Charlene's remains.

When the last group of children came through the social hall for their snack, Andrew found Marilyn and told her that he was heading home. I'll have burgers on the grill when you get home."

"Thanks honey. That sounds wonderful. It has been a long day."

It was not terribly long after Andrew made it home that Marilyn and Charlotte pulled into the drive. Andrew already had the hamburgers on the grill. It would be hard for someone not to smell the aroma that filled the air.

Marilyn walked up to Andrew. With his back against her front, she put her arms around his waist. She looked at the grill for a moment. "Are you planning to feed an army this evening?" She inquired.

Andrew laughed. "No sweetheart! I thought I would throw an extra burger or two on the flames. I have a funny feeling we may company over for dinner."

Whispers in the Willows

"Oh! Did you invite some of your colleagues over?" She asked.

"Nope!" Andrew said confidently. "I have a hunch that Woody will be joining us."

"How can you be so sure?" Marilyn was startled when she heard someone start to step up to the porch. She was shocked when she turned and saw Woody standing behind them.

"Mr. Woody! Did you come for dinner?" Woody politely smiled at Marilyn and took his seat at the picnic table. Marilyn could not help but feel compassion for Woody. Even she was starting to believe he was part of their family.

Charlotte ran up to him with a smile on her face. She scrambled onto the chair next to him and proceeded to tell him the story of Jonah and the Whale. "I learned all about him today at church!"

Woody listened attentively as Charlie shared the story she learned that evening. His eyes sparkled with new life as he stared at this little princess sitting next to him. "Mr. Woody?" Charlie stopped her story to ask one simple and innocent question.

"Yes. Miss Charlie." Woody answered.

"I want you to be my grandpa! Would you?"

Her little request ignited emotions in Woody that he kept inside for so long. Woody did what he did best. He wept.

"Why are you crying Mr. Woody?" Charlie wanted to know. She needed to know.

All Woody could say: "Charlie, my tears are born out of joy! We need to 'okay' your request with your mom and dad."

Marilyn saw the interaction between her little girl and Woody. She knew Charlie meant the world to Woody. She left the two on the porch and went to help Andrew bring dinner to the table. It was hard for Marilyn not to spill the beans about the work going on in the summer cottage. Andrew, on the other hand, talked a mile a minute about the river and the search for Charlene.

After dinner, Charlotte gave Woody a kiss goodnight. She sang him a song she learned in VBS.

"Goodnight Kiddo." Andrew said giving her a hug and a kiss.

Marilyn accompanied Charlotte to the bathroom while she took her bath and got ready for bed. She said her prayers and crawled under her covers. Her mother read her a story and turned out the light.

Whispers in the Willows

Before joining the men on the porch, Marilyn put on a pot of coffee and cut a few slices of pie. In the cool of the evening, the three enjoyed the warmth of friendship. When the pot of coffee was empty, Marilyn and Andrew insisted upon seeing Woody to his door.

As they bid Woody goodnight, he asked if they wanted to step in for a minute. "For a moment." Marilyn replied as she nudged Andrew forward. Marilyn was curious to see the inside of Woody's house for herself.

Dodging rotten boards on the porch steps, they stepped into Woody's living room. While it had a distinct odor, it did not smell as rancid as the kitchen. Woody invited them to sit down.

"I can't leave Charlotte. You understand."

"Another time Ms. Marilyn."

She nodded. "Another time Woodrow."

Most of the plaster from the ceiling was gone. Lathe boards were visible on the walls. Springs shot up through the cushions of his couch. There were piles of newspapers and magazines stacked in piles across the floor. The old wood floor had numerous splintered boards; various sized throw rugs buried the remains of a floor that shined with the sun, and that once was slick as ice. Dirty dishes blanketed the couch and coffee table. Flies buzzed around the dirty dishes. Fly paper strips hung from the ceiling. They were covered with dead flies and moths.

The room was dark and dingy. A single low watt bulb hung from a wire on the ceiling. It flickered like a flame on a candle. The windows in Woody's living room had panes of broken glass. The windows had planks of wood nailed across them.

"Did you see that living room? What filth! Deplorable!" Marilyn said in shock.

"Marilyn, he's an old man." Trying to cushion Marilyn's disdain and disgust, Andrew reasoned. "He can't help it."

"Andrew, that is not an excuse."

Remembering everything he witnessed in the past few days, Andrew had a hard time containing himself. "Marilyn, honey." He exclaimed. "Don't you think you are being a little too hard on him?"

Marilyn pondered for a moment. "You are right. It was my idea to help him."

Andrew was a person who did not show off his knowledge of the Bible. But, in this instance, his interpretation of the Scriptures beamed just as brightly as the stars in the heavens. Marilyn was impressed with what spewed out his mouth next.

"I cannot help but equate the life of Woody to that of Jonah. Both men lost something very valuable in the waters. For Jonah, it was his life and for Woody, it was everything that gave him reason to live. Both men\ bore the brunt from their experiences. Don't you think?"

Marilyn had a hard time digesting what Andrew said. It was profound, yet it was simple. "Sweetheart, I am so proud of you."

"Marilyn, let's not head in yet," Andrew said pulling Marilyn onto the swing. "Sit with me for awhile." Together they sat in silence taking in the beauty surrounding them. Andrew stared at the stars lost in thoughts about finding Charlene. Marilyn stared up at the starry night. For each star she saw in the night sky, she counted a blessing.

Chapter 30
"Why?"

The next several days were a whirlwind. Like an army of ants marching to and fro from their hill, work crews and contractors were in and out of Woody's back lot working on the summer cottage. Gary and Tommy worked on the car parked in Woody's driveway. Charlotte helped Woody pick vegetables from his garden and harvest fruits from his trees. Andrew worked with his engineers on the land surveys. And Marilyn made sure everyone had what was needed to keep the work moving forward.

"Hon, my mom called and wants Charlotte to come for a long weekend." Said Marilyn.

"That would be great Marilyn," Andrew responded. "Charlie would enjoy seeing them."

"They will get in Friday afternoon. After the VBS picnic, they are going to head home."

Charlotte was excited when Friday finally arrived. She drew a picture of herself and ran it over to Woody. "This is in case you forget what I look like when I'm gone."

Woody chuckled to himself. "Sweet Charlie, I would never forget that button nose of yours."

"Mr. Woody, do you want to meet my grandma? You would like her. And my grandpa too. They are old like you. Please don't be mad at me. You are still my grandpa too."

Charlotte insisted that her mother take the grandparents over to meet Woody. Marilyn compromised. "How about we invite Woodrow to come to the church picnic tonight?"

Marilyn jotted a note and sent Charlotte to deliver it. Reporting back to her mother, "He said he'd LOVE to come!"

With hat in hand, Woody greeted the Orr's at their front door. He was quickly introduced to Marilyn's parents and off they went to the church.

More than fifty years had passed since Woody stepped foot in the church. The last time he sat in those pews was on the day he laid Alice and Charlene to rest. He hesitated to take a step forward into the sanctuary. The cross that hung in front of the sanctuary had not changed in fifty years.

Like a magnetic charge, Woody was drawn to the cross. His mind started to run wildly. He could not contain or control his thoughts. He thought about the death he witnessed during the war and how death washed away everything important to him.

He tried so hard to contain every emotion that enveloped his heart. The only words that he could muster came from the cross. "Why?" His silent petitions soon became public as he continued to ask the same question over and over again. "Why? Why Alice and Charley? Why not, me?"

Preacher Dan happened to be walking into the sanctuary. He heard Woody's pleas for absolution. He heard Woody's prayers for peace. He knew this was a very tender moment and, yet, a time to resolve the hurt that struck at the core Woody's soul just as the harsh river stole his Alice and little Charley.

He was very sensitive to Woody's state of mind. He silently approached Woody from the rear and sat in the pew behind this old soldier of misfortune. He gently placed his hand on Woody's shoulder and softly spoke. "That's a fair question to ask. I would be seeking the same answer as you."

Woody turned his head to face this stranger. Wiping the tears from his face, Woody asked: "Really? I was told never to question God"

"God has given you permission to ask." The pastor said. "Even Jesus asked the same question on the Cross. He asked the question of 'Why?' He wanted to know how God could forsake Him in such a situation."

The minister had Woody's full attention. "He did?" Woody wanted to know more: he needed to know more.

Whispers in the Willows

"Yes, yes He did." Preacher Dan went on to explain. "You see, what most people do not realize is that if people don't ask the hard questions, then they deprive God of giving them an explanation. It seems to me that you have spent almost your entire life wanting to know and wondering how."

"You are right." Woody said. He was not sure what to make of this preacher. He clearly understood the depths of Woody's pain. He seemed to have an insight to Woody's soul.

"Woodrow." He added. "I cannot possibly imagine losing everything that meant so much to me or for that matter the world to me. It is hard for me to fathom what you have endured for so many years."

He took a second or two to collect his thoughts. Preacher Dan was very much aware that whatever he said next would either reel Woody in from the raging river or leave him dangling and drowning in its rushing flow.

"I look at the same Cross every morning wondering how was it that God could love the world so much that He offered His Son to suffer such a cruel death. And while I cannot even begin to give you an accurate explanation for such love, I can say this: God fully comprehends your pain. For He too lost a Son: His only Son. I am sure He has been waiting for this day for a long time. This evening, you took the first step to mending a broken heart."

Woody sat stunned and speechless. Never did he even ponder the possibility that God Himself grieved the loss of a child. And while a thousand thoughts rain through the circuitry of his mind, Woody clearly comprehended this one fact. God knew his pain. Finally, he learned that God could grieve as he grieved.

The children started to enter the sanctuary. Preacher Dan invited Woody to stop by the church any time he needed to talk to someone.

Chapter 31
"Divine Intervention"

Woody's mind wandered as he looked about his surroundings. The cross and the simplicity of the church was comforting. He watched Pastor Dan herd the children to the altar as they prepared for their closing production. Woody studied the congregants sitting in the sanctuary. "It can't be! It is. Is it?" Woody saw someone, or thought he saw someone he knew. Rising from his seat, he made his way down the center aisle and to the front of the church.

In the front pew sat Cheryl and her husband David. Their daughter was on the riser in the front of the church ready to sing with her VBS friends. Next to Cheryl sat her grand- father. Woody stood in front of their pew and looked down at the old man next to his great niece Cheryl. "Miller. Is that you Miller?" The old man in the pew looked up at Woody.

In the moment of recognition, old Mr. Miller started crying. Woody was crying. Mr. Miller stood up and the two men embraced. "Miller, Miller, my old friend." Woody cried out. Not many people in the church knew either man. All they saw were two old men embracing one another has if they were brothers returning home from war. But both the Orr's and Cheryl were conscious of the impact the embrace carried. Goosebumps sent a chill through Andrew.

"Marilyn, I prayed for divine intervention to get those two together. I just didn't think it would happen so soon."

Marilyn squeezed Andrew's hand. "I too was thankful for a speedy response to my petition for divine intervention. Only the Good Lord could orchestrate this perfect encounter.

Woody sat next to his old time pal Miller. He had been called Miller from the time he and Woody were four or five years old. Woody couldn't remember Miller's first name.

Woody and Miller sat arm in arm throughout the closing program. Woody sang along to some of the songs he recalled from his youth.

When the program was over, Cheryl introduced Woody to her daughter Lissa. Marilyn and Andrew, along with Marilyn's parents joined the happy reunion as they made their way to the social hall. Stories were told. Joys and sorrows were shared. It was an evening for renewal, both spiritual and heartfelt.

Marilyn's parents excused themselves. They had a long drive ahead of them. Charlotte gave hugs and kisses to her parents and to Woody and then she was off with her grandparents for a few days in Elbow Lake.

Cheryl promised her grandfather that she would make sure to take him to Woody's once a week for a visit.

Whispers in the Willows

Woody and Miller hugged and promised to stay in touch between visits with phone calls. They said their goodbyes. Woody hopped into the Orr's car feeling like a new person.

"There are no words to describe the joy in my heart." Woody said.

"We are so happy you came tonight. You are a dear sweet man and you have so much living left to do." Marilyn replied.

"Would you kind folks like to join me for a night cap before turning in?" Woody asked. Marilyn looked at Andrew. Andrew looked at Marilyn. Neither one knew how to reply. "I know my place ain't pretty. I sure wished I would have taken better care of my little princess's home."

Andrew thanked Woody for the invitation but told him they would take a rain check.

"I've got some studying to do tonight anyhow." Woody told Andrew. Andrew gave him a puzzled look.

"Ace that test Woody." Andrew said chuckling. Woody gave a salute and disappeared into his house.

Chapter 32
"Woody Is Off to the Woods"

That evening, Andrew decided to stay up and survey the flow of the river fifty years ago. He sat there in his dining room studying the prints of antiquity. He tried to muster in his mind where Charlene's remains now rest.

He looked out his window. He could see the flickering of the one light illuminating Woody's living room. It seemed that Woody himself was doing a little calculating of his own. Andrew noticed that Woody was kneeling down on his floor studying something. It appeared that Woody was plotting papers on his floor. Andrew was not aware of Woody's ability to commit certain things to memory.

Though an old man, Woody was trained to survey landscapes unfamiliar to him. He saw the prints from the past. Woody made it a point to memorize every detail of those old drawings. As Andrew was trying to figure the flow of the water fifty years ago, so too was Woody.

Andrew's attention was diverted as he looked down at the papers now scattered across his table. When he looked down, something seemed to shed light on where Charlene could have possibly been laid to rest. "That's it!" He shouted.

Whispers in the Willows

He looked hard left and noticed Woody was no longer in the living room. At first, Andrew thought Woody retired for the evening. His instincts were wrong. He miscalculated Woody's ability to retrieve information. He heard Woody's front door slam and saw him leaving his premises with a flashlight in hand.

"Oh, no!" Andrew thought. "I pray you are not doing what I believe you are doing!"

Andrew's worse fears became a reality. He followed Woody's every motion. He watched Woody walk toward the back yard and grab one of the boy's shovels. Woody straddled the instrument for digging over his shoulder as if he were holding a rifle. In the darkness Woody disappeared with light in hand and shovel resting comfortably on shoulder.

"For heaven's sake, Woody! Not now." Andrew was beside himself. He was not sure what to do or how to do it. He did not want Woody walking through the woods by himself. At first, he thought about getting in his car to follow Woody. But the glare from the headlights may alert Woody of Andrew. As a result, Andrew believed it best to follow Woody by foot.

He ran to his garage, snatched a flashlight from the shelf, and started to track Woody. Andrew had a hard time accepting how such an old man could be so elusive and evasive. Many times Andrew would blurt from under his breath: "Woody, where are you?"

Before he knew it, Andrew was lost in the woods that he now trod. Fear overwhelmed him. He was not accustomed to marching around in the darkness and he was not acclimated to the many challenges he now faced. He could hear the howls of the coyotes as their cries broke the silence of the night air. He could begin to hear the owls hooting as they woke up and he could feel his heart start to rapidly pound. He was alone. He was lost. But most importantly, he was afraid.

He heard some shuffling of the leaves from the abyss. His faith intensified. He prayed like he never prayed before. He believed he had come to his end. Suddenly, he saw a light shine from nowhere. He heard a voice. It was a familiar voice. It was a somewhat welcoming voice. It was Woody's voice.

"Son!" Woody sternly said. "What are you trying to do, get yourself killed?" Woody added. "Did you not know there are animals out here that would love to eat you alive."

With horror written all over his face, Andrew replied: "I am starting to realize it, now."

Woody shined his light toward Andrew. "Are you following me? Look, I may not remember how to drive a car, but I sure do remember how to read charts. I know where Charlene is." He shouted.

Whispers in the Willows

Andrew still in shock looked at Woody only to question: "Are you trying to invite all the animals to our location?"

Woody laughed. "They already now where we are. Are you scared?"

"Maybe!" Andrew replied. "Can't this wait until tomorrow morning?"

"Well! I guess it is going to have to now. I need to get you home before you hurt yourself." Woody said with an air of confidence. "Pretty impressive for an old man, don't you think?"

"Quite impressive!" Andrew had to admit.

"I haven't lost a step in over fifty years." Woody chuckled. "Let me get you home so I can tuck you into bed." Woody finally had an upper-edge on his young neighbor.

Andrew was compliant. "I am not a position to argue at this particular point in time."

Chapter 33
"Charley, Here We Come"

"Why don't you come for breakfast in the morning," Andrew said to Woody. "We'll fuel up and then head to the river together." Andrew put his arm on Woody's shoulder. "Men didn't have the equipment and technology fifty years ago. We will find your Charley." The two men bid goodnight. Woody went home. Andrew went to Marilyn.

The smell of bacon tantalized Woody's nose. The aroma flowed through the broken windowpanes and into his living room. Woody went to the bathroom to freshen up.

Woody's bathroom had two large buckets. One bucket was used for waste. The other one was full of fresh water hauled up from the river that ran through the back of Woody's property.

The water pipes from Woody's well to the house broke decades ago. Woody either collected fresh water in rain barrels, or he had to haul it from the river behind his house. Without running water, Woody's toilets would not flush. He used buckets to do his business in and emptied them every couple days. He was used to the smell so he never noticed when the buckets needed to be dumped. He just figured it into his weekly routine. Mondays and Thursdays were the days he dumped waste buckets and refilled water buckets.

Whispers in the Willows

"Come on in." He heard Andrew say before he had a chance to knock on the door.

Woody took a seat at the table. It was a sight for sore eyes, and a hungry belly. After the blessing, they dug in.

Andrew had to run into work for a few hours. Marilyn duped Woody into accompanying her to the local hardware store under the pretense of helping her pick out paint for her house. After purchasing the gallons of the colors Woody preferred, she took him to the furniture store for his opinion on a new sofa. She encouraged Woody to test out different mattresses. And then she sought his opinion on other household accessories.

Now Woody was itching to get to the river. He had an idea of where his little girl lay, and he wanted to get to her. He thought it was pure hogwash to be furniture shopping with Marilyn, but Woody did not want to let his friend down. After placing an order for new furniture, Marilyn and Woody headed back towards home.

Andrew was waiting for them. He was equipped with waders, shovels, and a small excavator sitting on a flat bed truck.

"Holy smokes!" Woody gasped. Waving his boney finger at Marilyn "What was all that nonsense about?"

Woody was like a little kid at Christmas time. He begged Andrew to let him climb into the cab of the excavator. Remembering the driving lesson, "DON'T touch a thing!"

"I won't, I won't." Woody scaled the side of the flat bed and took a seat inside the digger.

As if he could read Woody's mind, Andrew conceded. "Fine." Andrew firmly said. You can ride back here, but I mean it."

"Yeah, I know, I know." Woody interrupted. "Don't touch nothing."

Marilyn climbed into the passenger seat of the flatbed and they headed towards the river. A few of Andrew's colleagues were already there. Andrew had to make sure to protect the integrity of the river while they shoveled and moved dirt.

On foot, Marilyn and Woody went down the left bank of the river. They used rakes and shovels to push aside overgrowth. Every few feet they overturned dirt looking for remains.

A pair of engineers put on waders and walked in the shallow edge of the river itself. They too had shovels and would periodically turn a pile of the riverbed over looking for something; anything.

Andrew and another set off down the right side of the river, leaving Henry to man the excavator. The excavator

Whispers in the Willows

would be a last resort. Andrew didn't want to alter the river if he didn't have to.

They worked tirelessly for several hours combing over a small area of land. "I don't' get it." Andrew said. "She should be here."

Consoling her husband, Marilyn had to remind Andrew of some harsh realities. "Andrew, it is possible a wild animal drug her away. She could have a final resting place nowhere near here. There are a lot of variables that could have come into play."

Andrew pulled out the survey maps. "What am I missing?" He scratched his head and studied the map, looked at the land, and studied the map some more. Frustration was setting in. But, like a flip of a switch, a light bulb clicked.

"You idiot." He thought to himself. "I'm so stupid." Andrew yelled out in frustration. "We are working off the wrong bridge. We need to be a mile down river by the old stone bridge." Pointing to the bridge in the background, "This bridge did not exist fifty years ago."

The crew packed up and headed a mile down river. They began their search and recovery efforts once again. They searched for about an hour when the crew heard a sound that made everyone stop dead in their tracks. Three short blasts from a whistle echoed down river. Three short blasts from a whistle was the announcement that remains had been unearthed.

Chapter 34
"You Got to be Kidding"

Those who heard the sound of the whistle stopped everything they were doing. They looked in the direction of the blasts and started to sprint to the spot where the others had already starting the excavation. Henry sat behind the miniature hoe and carefully scooped up the soil. Some sifted through the dirt that rested in the bucket, while the others took their shovels to sift through the loosened earth.

Hopes were running high for everyone: everyone but Woody. His attention was pulled in a different direction. Of course, he had a little help from the authorities high above. He could feel something tugging at him. Though he tried to concentrate on the work being done, the sensation of being pulled persisted. The last time Woody recalled such a feeling was when little Charley was in need of his attention.

Woody eventually caved in to this calling. He looked up and out. There in the distance he saw something that stood out like a sore thumb. Standing alone in the open fields was a Weeping Willow. "It can't be." He thought. "How could anyone have missed it? How did I miss it?" Woody was angry at his ignorance and his oversight.

In the midst of all the chaos and the mess of all the confusion, Woody was able to slip away unnoticed.

Resting on his shoulder was a shovel. With every step, Woody tears intensified. "Daddy's coming, sweetie. Daddy's coming."

Everybody back at what they believed to be Charlene's burial site cheered every time a bone was unearthed. Initially, they resembled the ribs of a small child. It was not until they came to the rest of the remains that their hopes in finding Charley drowned. What they discovered was nothing more than remnants of what was once a young bobcat.

Out of frustration, one of the younger workers blurted out: "This is a waste of my time. It is a waste of everybody's time." His remarks were ignored until he took his comments one step too far. "She is dead. She had been dead for fifty years. When will the old man ever get over it?"

There was complete silence. A storm was forming. What the young man did not know, as well as the others, was that the clouds rapidly rolling were not visible to the naked eye. It was brewing and blowing in Andrew's mind. Andrew was tired, he was exhausted, and he was not fond of this young man's attitude.

Like a tornado that rips across the landscape, Andrew tore through the crowds. He planted the young man to the ground, where he positioned the young man's face in the dirt that was recently disturbed. "Son." Andrew shouted. "If you do not expect to become one with the earth, then I would strongly suggest you keep your mouth shut."

Henry, in an attempt to do damage control before the winds of Andrew's temper did anymore harm, jumped out of the excavator and pulled Andrew off the young man. "Andrew, that's enough!" Henry shouted and then calmly stated: "That is not going to solve anything. He's still has a lot to learn. He still has a lot of living to do as well."

Henry then lifted Andrew off the young man. He straightened Andrew's shirt and reminded him. "We still have work to do. We have a little girl to find." He then added: "Don't get distracted from our original goal. It is to find a life lost: it is not to end someone else's life."

Drawing a deep breath, Andrew affirmed everything Henry just said. "You are right." He then stretched out his hand toward the young man on the ground. "My apologies. Let me help you up."

The young man graciously accepted Andrew's plea for forgiveness and unbelievably, allowed Andrew to pull him to his feet. "Sir." The young man said. "I should be the one apologizing to you and those working to find this man's little girl."

Andrew started to scope the crowd. Woody was nowhere to be found. Still shaking from his little temper-tantrum,

Andrew had a look of confusion. "By the way, where in the world is Woody?"

Everyone started to look at one another. Woody was nowhere to be found. "Great!" Andrew said in frustration. "Now we have two people to find."

The workers started to scour the land. One of them spotted Woody in the distant. He was nothing more than a small blip on the radar. Woody was walking slowly and steadily to the Weeping Willow that stood alone. "There he is!"

"How could we miss it?" Andrew thought.

Chapter 35
"Woody by the Weeping Willow"

Woody gained considerable ground since he excused himself from the excavating crew. The closer he walked to the Weeping Willow, the smaller his steps became. He cautiously advanced this hallowed ground. He knew Charley was soon to be unearthed.

He fell to his knees. He wept like he never wept before. "My baby girl. Daddy is here to take you home. Please tell me where to start." His reached out to remove some of the foliage that loosely lay around the tree. Woody squinted. "It can't be." He looked up toward the heavens only to say: "Thank you."

What he saw piercing through the soil was a hand of the doll he purchased for his Charley for her last birthday. Woody did not hesitate to begin the long tedious process of retrieving his little girl from her resting place. The moment his spade hit the soil, the evidence buried for so long became apparent.

The first thing Woody uncovered was the doll whose finger showed him the way. The clothing that laced her porcelain body was still intact. Her eyes were wide open as if to welcome Woody. And she was still smiling as if her father found her.

Whispers in the Willows

Woody carefully started to brush the dirt off this baby doll. What he witnessed next sent a series of shockwaves through Woody's central nervous system. He trembled uncontrollably. For before his very eyes, he saw the skeletal features of Charley's fingers tightly clutched around her baby doll. He leaned forward placing his hands on his Charley's. His only strength was to weep.

With his knees firmly planted to the ground, and his hands now lying atop of his little girl, Woody pleaded and he prayed. He finally found his little Charley. "Daddy has missed you for so long!" He cried aloud.

The workers advanced on Woody without notice. Woody was in his own world. He was reacquainting himself to the remains found. There was not a dry eye when the volunteers came upon the scene. Marilyn with so much tender care walked up to this wounded warrior: this wounded father. She placed her hands ever so gently on his shoulders and tearfully said: "You found her! Woody, you found her."

Woody did everything in his power to get to his feet, but whatever strength he had was lost. Andrew and Marilyn came to aid. They came to his side. They took hold of his elbows and said: "Come on Woody. These men will finish what you started. They will take care of your little girl."

Standing on his two feet, Woody, of all people, planted his face in Andrew's shoulder. "My baby!" He sobbed. "I found my baby!"

"I know, Woody." Andrew said reaffirming Woody's state of emotions. "I know. You found your baby." For a person who almost ended a life some time ago, Andrew demonstrated another side of himself to everyone watching. It was the side of him that drew Marilyn to him so long ago. It was the side of love.

Andrew asked everyone to please give Woody some time to grieve. Out of their respect for both the living and the dead, everyone stepped aside. Woody summoned Andrew and Marilyn to remain as he continued to stare upon Charley's remains.

Moments turned into minutes, and minutes were quickly elapsing into evening. Andrew and Marilyn escorted Woody to a safe place for him to sit. "Woody. These men have to finish uncovering your baby." Moved by everything that took place, the young man who made the derogatory comments hours before, stepped up and volunteered to continue digging in honor of Woody's daughter.

Chapter 36
"A Care Package"

The sheriff was summoned to the scene. He arrived with the coroner. They thanked everyone for their help and said that they would handle things from there. "Woody, you go on home now and let us do our job. Charlene's remains will be taken to the funeral parlor. You can make final arrangements with them in the morning."

Woody did not want to go. The sheriff handed Marilyn the baby doll and asked for her help in getting Woody home. With much coaxing, Andrew put Woody in the passenger seat of the flatbed and Marilyn squeezed in between he and Andrew. Other than Woody's muffled crying, it was a quiet ride back to the farmhouse.

Andrew pulled the rig into the back of his property. "I'll take it back in the morning." He said. Although exhausted, Marilyn invited Woody in for coffee. He declined and said that he wished to be alone. Andrew watched as Woody crossed through the yard and disappeared into his house. Illuminating the rooms as he walked through them, Andrew watched Woody's silhouette pass by the windows. His stature slumped. His head hung low.

The one thing that Woody wanted most from life was to know what happened to Charlene. Now that he had closure, Andrew hoped Woody would maintain his will to live.

Marilyn filled a tub with sudsy water and put the porcelain doll in the water. Though the doll's clothes were intact, they were dirty. Marilyn laid the doll's dress on a thick towel and gently poured water over it until the water ran clean. She laid the dress by an open window so the evening breeze could dry it. She wiped the doll clean and dried her off.

"Marilyn, I think Woody needs that doll tonight."

"But the clothes are all wet Andrew."

"I don't think he will care about a wet dress. Can you put that doll back together so he can have it now?"

Marilyn retrieved a shoebox from her closet. She put the doll in the box along with a ham sandwich and a slice of pie. She then pulled a prayer card out of her Bible and tucked it in with the doll.

"Thank you for putting this together for Woody. I think it will bring him comfort." Andrew winked at his wife and set off next door.

Woody did not answer the knock at the door. Andrew pushed the door ajar. "I don't mean to seem ungrateful, but I just want to be alone. Please go away." Woody said in sorrow.

Andrew set the box on Woody's kitchen counter. "Woody, Marilyn fixed you a care package. Peace."

Andrew watched from his porch as Woody's figure made its way from the living room to the kitchen. Woody picked up the box Andrew left on the counter and stared at the doll.

Caressing the doll like a newborn baby, Woody curled up on his couch and fell asleep.

Chapter 37
"Here We Go Again!"

With a book in hand, Marilyn joined Andrew on the porch. The night was chilly for mid-summer. She wrapped a shawl around her shoulders and sat on the swing.

"May I join you?" He asked. "What book are you reading now?"

"It's called 'Killing Me Softly.' I found it buried beneath all the other books when I was rummaging around for a shoebox. I love the scene on the cover. It looks like a good read." Batting her eyes at Andrews, she added:" According to the authors, it is a romance for the ages."

Romance was something Marilyn and Andrew had failed to work on in the past several months. Andrew sat next to his beautiful wife hoping to spark a little flame and fling for the evening. With Charlie at her grandparents and Woody's Charley now found, maybe life could return to some form of normal.

Andrew stretched his arms as if to yawn, only to embrace Marilyn with his left arm. He carefully removed the novel from Marilyn's hands, closed it and set it on the swing. He used his right hand to direct her attention to him. This was a move Marilyn described as the "Andrew move." She understood all to well what was going through his mind.

Though she was just as exhausted as everyone else, she did not object. There was no opposition on her part. She helped Andrew execute a play from his former playbook by meeting his lips halfway. Both could feel the intensity from such a powerful punch. Marilyn whispered: "Why Mr. Orr, if I didn't know any better, I would think..."

Her thought was rather rudely interrupted as a loud clap of thunder rattled the windows. A storm was kicking up. In the distance they could hear thunder begin to beat its drum. It rolled and rumbled across the skies like a mighty locomotive. Lighting soon joined in the celebration. Bolts started to dance across the darkened skies only to make the landscape its floor.

The branches of the weeping willows swayed in the wind. Their music was haunting. "We better get inside." Marilyn said. "Oh Andrew! Stop your pouting. Who said we were finished?"

For a moment, she thought a bolt of lightning struck him as his face was electrically charged. His smile said it all. "I will meet you upstairs?"

There is nothing more spectacular than when the electrons and neutrons become excitedly charged. The energy it produces is beyond belief. Especially when a couple has been caught in a drought for some time. What Andrew and Marilyn were quick to learn: storms can turn ugly. The direction a person believes it to be heading can turn without fair warning.

The winds started to gain momentum across the prairies. Rain started to pelt the side of the house and started to penetrate through the open windows.

"I'll be up in a moment, sweetheart." Andrew sang with words of praise. "I need to close the windows down here."

Marilyn smiled: "You will know where to find me!"

Andrew could not move fast enough across the first floor shutting one window to the next. He was definitely on a mission: that is, until he looked out and saw a flashlight breaking through the raindrops. It came from Woody's front porch. Andrew could see the light move in motion as Woody marched off his front porch and into the dark and stormy night.

"Oh, no!" Andrew said disappointedly. "Not again! Woody, what are you doing? Where are you going?"

From their bedroom, Marilyn came rushing down the steps, all the while draping herself with a robe. "What's going on?" She inquired.

"It's Woody!" Andrew said in anger. "He is at it again."

Whispers in the Willows

"At what?" Marilyn was completely unaware of everything that transpired the night before.

"I believe he is on a death march!" Andrew sounded off. "I should let him finally make peace with the world."

Marilyn slapped Andrew across the arm. "You cannot let him walk in this storm!" She blurted. "You need to go after him."

Like a child who was denied his request to spend the night at a friend's house, Andrew cried: "Do I have to?" Marilyn's robe outlined every detail of her figure, and easily distracted Andrew from his friend next door. However, he did not have to wait for the answer, he could tell from Marilyn's expression.

"Okay!" He pouted. "Woody, you owe me!" Andrew grabbed some rain gear, a flashlight and a pair of boots. Though he could figure out where Woody was heading, he would have to follow on foot. His car was at the field office. Marilyn's car was blocked in by the flatbed he borrowed from work. He did not have the time to switch vehicles around.

He hastily kissed Marilyn and was off to find Woody wandering in the wilderness. There was something about Woody most people never completely understood. He was used to walking through such a hostile environment. Decades ago when came he home from the war; the war also came home with him. There were certain aspects about his European tour he never let go or let loose. Tracking under the most volatile situations was one of them.

Rather than following the beaten path behind their homes, Andrew raced along the roads. His age worked in his favor. While Woody still maintained his sense of coordination and his skills from scouring across the countryside, Andrew had agility on his side.

He did, albeit, have a hard time running against the wind. Many times he believed he too was going to become a casualty. He tried to protect his face from the rain that blew horizontally, but to no avail. "Woody!" He murmured out loud every time his face was pounded by hail.

When he finally made it to his destination, he saw Woody standing next to the guardrail of the bridge. With a flashlight in one hand and Charley's doll in the other, Andrew could hear Woody scream: "Daddy's coming! I will save you!"

"Woody!" Andrew, trying to break his voice through what Mother Nature threw at him, screamed. "Woody! Don't!"

Unfortunately, Andrew's words did not sink in to Woody's estranged mind. He was caught between three realms: the war of long ago; the mighty water that raged below, and his need to join his little girl. Woody started to scale the guardrail, when from out of nowhere he was pulled back by the back of his shirt.

"Not now!" Andrew said with an authoritative voice. "Not here! Your mission is not complete soldier."

Whatever Andrew said awakened and aroused Woody's conscious. "What do you mean it is not over, sir?" Andrew realized he was speaking in terms that Woody easily understood.

"You still have one more task to complete! I am ordering you to stand down!" He shouted in Woody's ear.

"Yes sir!" Woody respectfully responded. "What do you require of me, sir?"

"We have found Charley! She still needs for you to pay your final respects to her life." Andrew echoed.

"Fifty years ago tonight, sir." Woody replied.

"What happened fifty years ago this evening?" Andrew was at a loss.

"Fifty years ago this evening, I lost everything sir!" Woody started to weep. "It should have been me."

There both men stood. They were being pounced by everything that the storm could throw at them. Water was rushing down their faces like water spills off a mighty waterfall. They were drenched. And if they continued to stand still, they too would be drowned.

"But it wasn't!" Andrew said lowering his voice. "You were left to complete the task now before you, son."

"Please, tell me how?" Woody begged.

"Soldier." Andrew explained. "It is by living the life that those who lost their lives were never afforded to live. Now soldier, I want you to return to your barracks, and we will settle this matter in the morning."

"Yes, sir!" Woody sounded off. "Here, sir. Will you protect my baby." He relinquished the most valuable possession Woody had at the present. It was "Charley's " little doll. "It seems that I have done so for so many years."

"Your request has been respectfully granted." Andrew said. "Now soldier, I am ordering you to return from where you came!"

"Yes sir!" There was no barking or bickering on Woody's part. He faced the direction of his house and started his walk back. With Charley's doll still clasped in his hand, Andrew followed Woody every step of the way.

Chapter 38
"Charley's Coming Home"

After his breakfast, Andrew loaded up the borrowed tools on the back of the flatbed. Marilyn was getting her shoes on to accompany him on the ride.

Woody came through the broken fence and approached Andrew. Woody looked at Andrew and thanked him for making sure that he did not become another casualty to the strong currents. Somewhat embarrassed, Woody had to ask: "Can I have Charlie's doll back?" He then went on to make another petition. "Do you think you or the Misses could give me a ride to the funeral parlor this morning?" Woody inquired.

Andrew obliged to Woody's request. "No problem Woody. We would be happy to."

"Andrew," Marilyn called out the back door. "Oh good morning Woody." She said upon seeing Woody out back. "Charlotte is on the phone. Come say hello before you take off. I'm going to stay here and talk with Charlotte and my mom."

After chatting with Charlotte for a few moments, Andrew and Woody headed for town. The ride was quiet. Andrew dropped Woody off at Winston's Funeral Parlor and told him that he would be back for him once he dropped off his work vehicle.

Andrew was spent. He was exhausted. Outside of laying and surveying the future developments within this growing populace, he spent a better part of his time helping Woody find closure. He also thought about the missed opportunity he had with Marilyn that previous evening. But then again, Andrew underestimated the heart of a woman. He will soon learn that there was nothing more attractive than a man willing to sacrifice his all to save another.

In the meantime, Woody sheepishly and silently walked into the funeral home. Old Mr. Winston knew Woody would be walking through those doors. He had been around the town as long as Woody. He was retired and his two grandsons ran the family business. Old man Winston made a special trip into town to meet Woody today. He gave his old friend a hug and motioned for Woody to sit down.

Old Man Winston served Woody tea and coffee cake. The two men spent some time catching up before getting down to business. Woody expressed his intentions to Winston. "I'd like to have Charley buried on my property. Would that be possible?" Because there was no flesh and blood to decompose, old man Winston told Woody that he could bury Charlene at home. There were stipulations about using an appropriate container and soil depth; but yes, Woody would bring Charley home.

Mr. Winston called Preacher Dan to set a date and time for a memorial service. Woody thought it seemed silly to have a memorial service. Most people in the town had no idea who Charlene was. Most of Woody's friends had passed on. He had Miller and Winston and his great-niece Cheryl.

Andrew swung by and picked Woody up. On the ride home Woody filled Andrew in about the memorial service and the most important thing; Charley would be coming home.

Chapter 39
"Charley Honored"

Woody looked in the mirror and splashed cologne on. He straightened up his collar and tightened up his bow tie. His gray eyes were caught somewhere between sadness and joy.

He put on his hat and headed out the door. Marilyn greeted him as she and Andrew came out of their house. They got into Andrew's car and headed for the memorial service.

Charlotte was on her way home from visiting with her grandparents, but they were not expected to arrive until later that evening.

Woody was a bit surprised when they pulled into the tiny church's gravel parking lot. Every space was full. There were even cars parked in the meadow next to the church. Inside, it was just as crowded. There wasn't a vacant pew. The exception: the one in the front with a ribbon on the end.

Woody walked to the front of the church, turned and faced the congregation. "How can this be?" He wondered. "All these folks are here for my Charley?" Looking into the sea of faces, he nodded in acknowledgement. He tipped his head as he humbled himself before the town folk.

Whispers in the Willows

With a lump in his throat he approached Miller. "Miller, Miller you old coot." Mr. Miller stood and embraced his old friend. "Miller, come sit with me." Woody followed the Orr's into the front pew. Miller sat next to Woody.

On the altar was a tiny little casket. It looked more like a little square box. It was made from pink marble and adorned with gold cherubs. Inside were Charlene's remains. Next to the pink marble box was an easel. On the easel was a painting of Charlene. "What? How?" Woody cried out. The people attending the service watched in silence as Woody walked up to the portrait. Charlene looked exactly as Woody remembered her. Woody ran his fingers along her face. He bent down and kissed Charlene on her cheek.

Woody gazed upon the portrait as though it were Charlene standing there in front of him. He fixed his eyes on the signature in the corner: L. Miller. "Leo Miller." He said under his breath. Woody turned to ask Miller: "How?" He was startled to find Miller standing beside him. In his hand, the photograph that Woody had passed along to Marilyn many weeks prior. Miller was blessed with an artistic paintbrush.

"Thank you! Thank you for this gift Miller." Woody said crying into Leo's shoulder. Pastor Dan, standing off to the side of the altar, let the two men have their moment before stepping up to the podium. Pastor Dan spoke of love, friendship, and letting go. He preached about forgiveness, remorse, and the toll burdens bring upon people.

A lady from the choir sang a solo. Cheryl's daughter played Amazing Grace on the piano. Before his closing prayer, Pastor Dan invited Woody to join him in front of the church.

Chapter 40
"You Were Never Alone."

Preacher Dan and Woody had a few moments to exchange words before the ushers released everyone from the pews. Woody was not quite sure how to strike up a conversation with this man of God. On all accounts, Preacher Dan seemed to be on the up and up. On with one hand, he was reverent and respectful. The pastor knew how to reach out to people right where they were. He was Godly, yet genuine.

Woody never forgot the conversation the two shared in the sanctuary some days ago. As people started to filter out, Woody finally broke the silence that seemed to separate the two men. "Thank you, preacher." He said.

With all humility, Preacher Dan said: "I am greatly humbled." The pastor did a Woody. He started to weep. "I pray God showers you with a peace beyond all understanding."

Woody was moved by the pastor's sincerity. "Preacher." Woody confidently said. "For years, I believed I was alone. I lost hope in humanity."

"Woodrow." Preacher Dan said while wiping his eyes dry. "You were not alone. From what I understand, you chose to seclude yourself from society." He went on to explain. "I cannot tell you how many times your name came up in prayer and for prayer."

The preacher was somewhat hesitant when Woody reached into the front pocket of the hand me down jacket Andrew loaned; and handed him a jar. Preacher Dan was not exactly sure of its contents. All he could make out was a picture he had seen previously. It was a picture of Woody's little girl "Charley."

"This is a gift to the church." Woody explained. "Use it however you and your congregation see fit." Preacher Dan did not completely realize the extent of Woody's generosity until days later. He set the jar on the desk.

The following Sunday morning, it screamed out to him. He was astonished that Woody had given the church $10,000.00 in honor of his little girl. Preacher Dan looked up and gave thanks. His attitude of gratitude was not so much for the money bequeathed on the church, but more importantly, because Woody made it to the chapel that morning with Andrew, Marilyn, and Charlie.

Chapter 41
"What in Tarnation?"

Over the next few weeks, blessings were flourishing. The church received a much-needed financial boost from Woody. Miller and Woody had renewed their friendship. Charlotte was home from her visit with the grandparents. She had met several new playmates through church and now had friends that would come to her house for the afternoon, or she to their homes.

Charley rested in an adorned box sitting in Woody's shoddy living room. The ornate box and the portrait looked out of place.

Andrew was content in his new position at work. Tommy and Gary had Woody's old car running. The car was now sitting in a body shop a few towns away waiting for the final touches. And Marilyn had made several friends in town. She was happy with her lot in life. She felt blessed in her role as a mother and a wife. She joined a Women's Bible Study at church. Through scripture, she learned what it meant to have a gentle spirit. To be pleasing to God, she pleased her husband. The passion and love between them was reawakened.

A rather important blessing awaited Woody. Today was the day he would move into his updated and remodeled summer cottage. Many of the town folk volunteered their time and resources to present Woody with a safe and welcoming place to live.

Woody was not one for fanfare. It was agreed there would be no pomp and circumstance. Marilyn made herself at home in the living room of the little cottage. Tommy and his dad joined her. Charlotte skipped up the overgrown path that led to the main house and summoned Woody.

Charlotte could hardly contain herself. She was full of excitement and couldn't wait for Woody to move into his new place. Charlotte so desperately wanted to accept Woody's invitations to step inside his house and join him for a fresh fruit tart or a glass of lemonade. But because of the unsafe and unsanitary conditions, her parents forbid her entry into Woody's home. With Woody in the new place, she would be allowed to join her grandfather for a cup of tea or snack of vegetables from his garden.

"What in tarnation?" Woody said as Charlotte hurried him along the path. While the little summer cottage was visible from the Orr's farmhouse, it was not visible from Woody's house. Beyond an outbuilding and through some tall grass they passed. When Woody saw the little cottage he couldn't believe it.

Again, "What in tarnation?" Marilyn, Tommy, and Tommy's dad came out onto the little porch.

Whispers in the Willows

"Surprise!" They yelled.

"It's your new house Grandpa! Now I can come inside when you invite me over for treats!" Charlotte beamed.

Mr. Clifford moved toward Woody. "Hey sport, I think we need to get you out of that decrepit manor and get you moved in."

"You did this for me? You all have done enough. It is too much: just too much for this old man." Woody was overwhelmed. He cried. He laughed.

"Do you like it?" Charlotte squealed. "Come inside Grandpa!"

Woody walked from room to room. "Marilyn. Why, it isn't nice to fool your elders. This furniture! You had me believe it was for your place." Sinking down onto the couch he noticed the portrait of Charlene hanging over the fireplace. "What in tarnation? How did you get that here?" Spying the ornate marble container: "How?"

When Charlotte knocked on Woody's back door, Andrew snuck in through the front door and grabbed the box with Charley's remains along with the portrait. Cutting through his own yard, he raced back to the cottage before Charlotte and Woody arrived.

Woody was humbled. "I can't thank you folks enough."

"Grandpa, you have an extra bedroom for sleepovers!" Charlie exclaimed. The thought made him chuckle.

"Sleepovers." Woody's eyes sparkled. He had the perfect houseguest in mind. "I need to go make a phone call!" The smile on Woody's face couldn't get any bigger. Marilyn pointed Woody to the kitchen.

"Woody, you have a working phone in your new cottage." Marilyn said

"Excuse me for just a minute." Woody was giddy as he headed into the kitchen. After a few minutes, he shouted: "He's coming! He's coming!" Woody looked like a leprechaun dancing a jig.

"Who? What are you talking about Woody?" Andrew asked.

"Miller! Miller is moving in with me."

And so it was settled. Cheryl and David moved Leo from the Good Samaritan Convalescence Home and in with Woody. That summer Charlotte and Miller's great-granddaughter Lissa became best friends. The two girls would often sit on Woody's cottage porch playing dolls. The grandpas taught Charlotte and Lissa how to bait hooks and to fish in the little stream. They helped Woody tend his garden and looked forward to fall to harvest the pumpkins growing beside the gazebo.

Whispers in the Willows

Marilyn loved the sounds of laughter that drifted from Woody's porch into her open windows. The giggles from the girls coupled with the throaty laughter from the men. Andrew enjoyed his visits to Woody's front porch as well. Woody and Miller would argue over a game of checkers while Andrew kicked his feet up and smoked his pipe.

On the days that Andrew was at work and Charlotte was off at a friend's house, Marilyn found herself meandering through Woody's property. She often left a pie at his door. Woody and Miller were defined as drifters as they made their way through the Orr's property and continued their debates on Marilyn's porch swing.

Tommy, who was now driving, would stop by and take the two old buddies out for a ride in the fixed up car. With a car, he soon found himself a girlfriend and his visits were fewer and fewer.

The only issue left for resolve: what to do with Woody's dilapidated house.

Chapter 42
"New School, Old House, And Town Gossip"

Over the next year there was much construction happening in Park River. New roads were cut through the vast farmland. New houses went up, over night it seemed. A new wing was added to the elementary school and there was talk about building a high school as well.

Woody, still in good health and enjoying life in his cozy cottage with his best friend, caught wind about the possibility of a high school for Park River. With Miller's help, together they dug up the mason jars buried on his property and Woody donated it to the school board.

Woody was bestowed the honor of shoveling the first scoop of dirt at the ground breaking ceremony for the Woodrow Elliot High School. In a matching hard hat, Charlotte stood next to him.

Marilyn was thankful that they lived away from the sprawl of new houses. She liked her little farm on the dead end road. Zoning prohibited building on most of the soil around the farm. But the Orr's did not completely escape the construction. Woody's house next door had been gutted. There was a flurry of activity as the house was restored to the grandeur it once displayed.

Whispers in the Willows

Many speculated as to who was moving in. Some folks said it was the mayor. Others thought perhaps Mr. Clifford. A few church gossips said it was Pastor Dan. They tsk tsk'ed the thought of the pastor moving into such an excessive place. "What happened to his vow of simplicity." The gossips said. But it wasn't Pastor Dan either.

Chapter 43
"Companion Plants Create Harmony."

"I missed you Grandpa Woody." Charlotte said throwing her arms around Woody. "Did you miss me?" She asked all out of breath. Today was the first day of summer vacation. Charlotte completed her kindergarten year and was out for the summer. She ran over to Woody's place to help him plant his summer garden.

It was also moving day. Today was the day everyone had been anticipating. Cars lined up down the dead end road. Everyone waited to catch a glimpse of the home's new occupants.

Marilyn and Andrew were just as curious as the rest of the town. Woody had been tight-lipped. They sat on their porch and watched as the U-Haul pulled in next door. "Hi neighbor!" A familiar voice rang out.

"Oh my word! Cheryl?" Marilyn declared. "You and David bought Woody's house?" She asked surprised.

Lissa darted into the Orr's front yard. "Is Charlie home?" She asked.

"She's out back with the grandpas honey." Marilyn answered. Lissa took off towards the cottage.

Andrew walked over to the truck and offered his help to unload.

Cheryl came and sat on the step next to Marilyn. "Woody gave us the house." She said. "He wished it to stay in the family. I'm his great-niece and he said I'd have a growing family and signed the deed over. I promised him that I would keep it in the family. He set up a trust that would cover the up-keep. I couldn't turn him down."

"I am thrilled to have you next door. Charlotte will be too. It will be nice to have adult female company."

"It will be nice being close to my grandfather." Cheryl said. "He's getting up there and with my parents living in the south, I'm all he's got."

"Your grandfather has been a God-send for Woody." Marilyn said. "I'm glad he left the convalescence home and moved in with Woody. They are two peas in a pod those two."

"Mommy, mommy, mommy!" The peaceful morning was interrupted when Charlotte came running through the side yard.

"Grandpa fell in the garden and won't get up." Charlotte cried.

"Where is Miller?" Marilyn asked.

"At the moving truck with Lissa." Charlotte replied.

With panic rising in her voice, Marilyn called out "Andrew! Andrew, something is wrong with Woody." Hearing the panic in her voice, Andrew ran toward the cottage. David, Cheryl, and Marilyn were right behind him.

Andrew knelt down next to Woody and gently shook him. "Woody, Woody, can you hear me?" He pled. Andrew checked for Woodys pulse. Marilyn stood trembling. Miller came up and put his arm around Cheryl.

"Go call for an ambulance!" Cheryl cried out loud breaking the silence that left everyone's heart just as still as Woody's.

Andrew shook his head. "He's gone." Tears streamed down Andrew's face."

There Woody lay. He was motionless. He was lifeless. His eyes that were once sunken and sullen stared unto the heavens. Nowthey beamed with new life as the rays of the sun broke through the portals of Woody's soul. Everyone could not help but notice the smile on Woody's face. The long hard battle he fought for so many years was now over. Though some may say he lost the battle, everyone agreed he won the war. He was at peace. He was now in the presence of his Lord and was finally reunited with those who had gone on before him: most notably his wife and daughter.

But that was not the only thing people noticed. For in Woody's right hand was Charley's doll. At the time no one understood the true significance the doll he still held onto so dearly..

"He's gone." Marilyn picked her daughter up and took her inside Woody's cottage.

"What's wrong with Grandpa?" Charlotte innocently asked her mother.

With a heavy heart Marilyn held Charlotte tight. "Honey, Woody's heart stopped. He died sweetheart." A tearful Charlotte buried her face into her mother's chest and cried.

Miller kissed his friend gently on the lips. "It was a good life. Thank you for including me."

David hugged Cheryl. "I'm sorry we won't get the chance to know Woody."

Andrew found a phone book. He called the sheriff and then he called Pastor Dan. Miller. Pastor Dan took the two little girls to the farmhouse and kept them occupied. Dave and Cheryl, with the help of some friends unloaded the U-Haul.

Marilyn and Andrew stayed with Woody. Marilyn held Woody's hand. Andrew held Marilyn. Through her tears Marilyn laughed, "Remember when we first moved here and you got so mad at me for befriending Woody."

"Remember how bad his house smelled." Andrew said back. "He sure was a lot of work wasn't he?"

While waiting for the ambulance to come for Woody, Marilyn and Andrew reminisced about their time with Woody as their neighbor. "Charlotte is going to be so heartbroken," Marilyn lamented. "She was excited for summer and spending time with Woody. I feel so bad for her."

Andrew stared off, "The kids at VBS are going to be sad. They loved having him as a teacher last summer."

Andrew hugged Marilyn a little harder. "Woody brought us closer together. I'm thankful for that." Andrew said.

Pastor Dan came through the fence. He embraced Andrew and then Marilyn. Knowing how close they were to Woody, he offered his condolences. After a brief discussion, it was decided that once Woody's body was dressed for burial, he would be buried on his property. They would place Charlotte's remains in the casket and bury father and daughter together.

The paramedics were about to lift Woody's body on the stretcher to transport him to the coroner's. Before so doing, they reached down to remove the doll firmly planted in Woody's hands. One paramedic gently undid each of Woody's fingers as he removed this precious item and gave it to Marilyn.

Marilyn noticed there was a letter that covered the doll's figure. She opened it only to read Woody's final words to the world. Within his message was a heart of gratitude to her and Andrew for never giving up on him and for restoring hope in the life he had remaining. The doll was to be given to Charlie. It was his gift to his granddaughter next door. She was to keep the doll as a token of his love for Charlie.

Marilyn wept as she read the letter out loud. After reading Woody's chicken scratched letter, Marilyn realized that Woody understood his time on earth was soon to pass. It dawned on her that he was attempting to wrap up any loose ends before his departure. She whispered under her breath: "You almost made it Woody."

Before his body was placed in the ambulance, Marilyn asked to have a moment with him. She started to stroke her long fingers through Woody's long gray hair. She looked upon the man's face that bore the brunt of so much pain and sorrow; yet whose heart was pure as gold. She leaned over to whisper in his ear: "I love you Woody. We love you." She concluded her time but softly pressing her subtle lips upon his cheek. "Goodbye my dear friend."

Woody's memorial service was held at the gazebo on the back of his property. Pastor Dan led the memorial for the few friends that were in attendance. Charlotte stuck a school picture in the coffin so that Woody would not be alone. Marilyn had the porcelain doll that was Woody's greatest treasure. Though Woody's instructions specifically stated the doll was to go to his "Charlie," Marilyn did not want him to be alone either. She to put the doll in the casket with Charlotte's picture.

As if Woody's spirit spoke to Charlie, Charlie stopped her mother dead in her tracks. "Mommy, can I keep the doll?" Charlotte asked. "It was special to Woody so it will be special to me."

Charlie's request reminded Marilyn of Woody's final message that draped the doll. ."Yes, sweetheart. You may keep the doll." Marilyn said giving her daughter a hug.

After the brief memorial service, Woody's was buried on the other side of the river that ran through the back of his property. Miller remained in the little cottage. The girls continued to visit Miller just as they did with Woody, but for Charlotte it was not the same.

There was a gaping hole in Charlotte's heart that could not be filled. There was a hole in Marilyn's heart. And Andrew missed his dear friend.

Over the summer, Charlotte tended to Woody's garden. Like the plants and the fruit trees that Charlotte tended, friendships and bonds were rooted in healthy soil and they yielded fruitful harvests. "Companion plants" Woody called them. "Companion plants create harmony in the garden as companions create harmony in one's life."

Woody's garden was laid out with meticulous thought. He knew which vegetables worked well together. Mint grew near the cabbage plants. The mint improved the flavor of the cabbage. Patches of herbs growing in between the rows of plants helped keep the pests away and heightened the flavor of the yield.

He also knew that some vegetables would not grow well next to other particular plants. Just as people may not get along with their neighbor, the same holds true for plants.

Just as the vegetable garden fed Woody, Woody nourished the lives of those he touched. He made sure his little plot of earth was home to the kind of companions that worked well with one another for the betterment of each individual.

The end.

Printed in the United States
By Bookmasters